Also in this series

Larryboy and the Hideous Horde

Larryboy and the Crusty Crew

ZONDERKIDZ
www.zonderkidz.com

Larryboy to the Rescue
ISBN 978-0310-73858-9

This title is also available as a Zondervan ebook.
Visit www.zondervan.com/ebooks

Requests for information should be addressed to:
Zonderkidz, 5300 Patterson Ave. SE, Grand Rapids, Michigan 49530

Written by Doug Peterson

Cover and Interior Illustrations: Michael Moore
Cover design and art direction: Big Idea Design, Paul Conrad, and Karen Poth
Interior design: Big Idea Design, Holli Leegwater, John Trent, and Karen Poth

Printed in the United States

13 14 15 16 17 18 19 20 21/DCI/ 15 14 13 12 11 10 9 8 7 6 5 4 3 2 1

3 books in 1

VeggieTales

LarryBoy
To The
Rescue

Doug Peterson

ZONDER**kidz**

VeggieTales

LARRYBOY™

IN THE AMAZING BRAIN-TWISTER

WRITTEN BY
DOUG PETERSON

ILLUSTRATED BY
MICHAEL MOORE

BASED ON THE HIT VIDEO SERIES: LARRYBOY
CREATED BY PHIL VISCHER
SERIES ADAPTED BY TOM BANCROFT

ZONDERkidz

ZONDERVAN.com/
AUTHORTRACKER
follow your favorite authors

TABLE OF CONTENTS

CHAPTER 1

TORNADO ALLEY
5:15 A.M.

There was something
strange in the air in Bumblyburg.
Black, ragged clouds hung low over the
city. The air had a greenish glow to it.
Thunder rumbled across the sky. It was still
very early on a Monday morning, so the streets
of Bumblyburg were almost empty. In fact, only a
single car moved through the downtown area.
Behind the wheel of that car was Officer Olaf, making his rounds.

"Somewhere...over the rainbow—"sang Officer Olaf
in his heavy Swedish accent. He loved to belt out
songs while listening to his favorite radio show—*The
Accordion Hit Parade,* doncha know?

Perhaps if the radio had been turned down lower,
he might have realized that something strange and
sinister was racing up from behind.

A tornado!

Pulling up to a red stoplight, Olaf continued to
cut loose in song. "We represent the lollipop kids!
The lollipop kids...!"

If the kindly policeman had just looked

into his rearview mirror, he would have seen the swirling mass of black, twisting clouds slip up behind him. It was probably the only tornado in history to ever stop at a red light.

When the light turned green, Olaf finally took a quick look into his rearview mirror.

"AHHHHHHHHHHHHH!" Officer Olaf made a screeching left turn. He was sure the tornado would continue to move straight. But here's the strange part...

The tornado made a sharp left turn, too.

Officer Olaf made a right turn.

The tornado made a right turn.

Officer Olaf increased his speed by twenty miles per hour.

So did the tornado.

Left turn, right turn, left turn!

He even made a complete turnaround and caused his squad car to flip up on two wheels, causing sparks to fly. But everything that Officer Olaf tried—failed. He couldn't shake this maniac monster of a tornado. It had to be the strangest car chase ever.

Officer Olaf suddenly remembered the old safety rule: never try to outrun a tornado in your car. So he brought his squad car to a screeching halt and tried to flee on foot—or whatever it is that vegetables flee on.

"Open up! Open up!" Olaf pounded on the door to the Shave and Shine Barber Shop. He needed to find a storm cellar fast! But the shop wasn't open yet. Olaf sprinted up Bumbly Boulevard, made a quick right turn, and found himself trapped in an alley—a dead-end alley. His heart sank as he stared up at the large brick wall in front of him.

The tornado turned into the alley, moving slowly toward him—like a monster that knew its victim was trapped.

CHAPTER 2

TWISTER!

6:45 A.M.

Meanwhile, in another part of Bumblyburg...
Larry the Cucumber loved rainy days and
Mondays. Why else would he get up extra early
just to play games before work?

"Left hand red, right hand green," said Archie, after
twirling a spinner. Archie was Larry's trusted butler.

Larry stood on a plastic mat, which was covered
with colored circles. He and Archie were beginning to
play the classic game Twister. But something didn't
seem quite right.

"What did you just say, Archie?" Larry asked.

"The spinner says to put your left hand on red,
your right hand on green."

Larry blinked a few times. He looked down at his
sides. "This isn't working, Archie."

But there was no time to think about that now.
A spotlight shot into the air, placing the
Larryboy emblem high in the dark, stormy sky.
And that meant only one thing. There was
trouble in Bumblyburg.

"I still say that a pager
would be an

easier way to reach me," said Larry, as Archie dialed the phone to find out what was wrong in the city.

"There's a robbery in progress at Mr. Snappy's Extremely Gigantic Toy Emporium," Archie exclaimed, hanging up the phone. "Quick! Not a moment to lose!"

Faster than lightning, Larry threw on his Larryboy costume, flossed his teeth with Larryfloss, slid down the Larrypole, leaped into the Larrymobile, clicked on his Larryseatbelts, and made sure his Larrymug was secure in the cup holder.

The Larrymobile raced out into the storm.

With weather-warning sirens blaring, the streets of Bumblyburg were still deserted. The only sign of life was at Mr. Snappy's Extremely Gigantic Toy Emporium, where an armored car was parked.

Larryboy leaped out of the Larrymobile and pushed his keyless-entry remote control. "Excuse me, Larryboy. But you've just set the car to self-destruct in ten minutes," the car computer told him. (Archie had equipped the Larrymobile with a computer that could talk. Larryboy called the computer Fred.)

"Peanut brittle," said Larryboy. "Thanks for the warning, Fred." Our plunger-headed hero pushed another button on his keyless remote and the Larrymobile was instantly transformed into a boat.

"Wrong button again," said Fred. "Or were you planning a moonlit cruise down Main Street?"

"Sarcasm from a computer?" Larryboy asked.

"The wonders of technology," Fred added.

After Larryboy finally pressed the correct button, the

Larrymobile switched back into a car and all of the locks clicked into place.

"Have a nice day. Be home by lunchtime," Fred told him as Larryboy bounded off.

It didn't take long for our hero to figure out what the trouble was. Somebody was stealing stuffed animals from the toy store and loading them into the armored car.

"Halt, toy napper!" declared Larryboy, as he jumped onto the roof of the armored car and struck a dramatic pose.

"Is that you, Larryboy?" came a voice from inside the armored car. Officer Olaf leaped out the side door.

"Officer Olaf?"

"Ya, it's true. You betcha, it's me," he said with a kindly twinkle in his eye.

Larryboy gave Olaf a puzzled look. "Your voice sounds a little deeper than usual."

"Just a cold," said Olaf. "It's going around, doncha know?"

Larryboy peered into the armored car, which was half-packed with stuffed animals.

"I don't understand," Larryboy observed. "Why all the toys?"

"Oh, it's really quite simple. We've been tipped off that a master criminal is going to try to steal stuffed animals from the toy store this very day. So I'm putting them into the armored car for safekeeping."

"Good idea!" Larryboy glanced back at the store, where piles of stuffed animals were waiting to be loaded into the car—like animals about to enter the ark. "Here, let me help you!"

"Much obliged, Larryboy."

For the next ten minutes, our superhero helped the policeman load up the car. "Another good deed done," said Larryboy, feeling pleased with himself as the armored car raced away.

Unfortunately, Larryboy didn't take a good, hard look at the license plate on that armored car. If he had, maybe he would have realized that something wasn't quite right about Officer Olaf—besides his strange voice.

The license plate read FOUL PLAY.

CHAPTER 3

OLAFS ALL OVER THE PLACE

7:23 A.M.

Larryboy
began the drive back to the
Larrycave. But as he pulled away from
the toy store, he accidentally pushed the
back-seat-driver button on Fred the Computer.
"You're driving too fast!" screeched Fred.
"Watch out for that fire hydrant! Slow down! Put
on your Larryblinker! How about some air conditioning back here?"

It took a few minutes, but a frantic Larryboy
finally figured out how to switch Fred back to normal.
Even Fred seemed relieved.

"Don't ever do that to me again," Fred scolded.
"And while you're at it, Larryboy, I'd swing by the
Bumblyburg police station."

"Why?"

"There's trouble with a capital *T*. And that rhymes
with *P*. And that stands for police station."

"What kind of trouble?" asked Larryboy.

"Don't ask me. I'm a computer, not a genius."

Turning his car around, Larryboy drove
straight for the police station.

Fred was right. Something definitely was going on. Several burly policemen were dragging a plum out of the station, but he wasn't going quietly.

"I may look like a plum, but I'm *Officer Olaf,* I tell you! I *work* here!" the plum shouted. "Take your hands off me!"

The policemen gave each other knowing glances. This plum was clearly off his rocker.

The plum claimed to be Officer Olaf and even sounded like the Swedish policeman, but he sure didn't look like Olaf. He was dressed like a scientist. He wore a white lab coat, complete with a pocket protector for his pens, and huge, thick, black-rimmed glasses. On the glasses were all sorts of blinking lights and gadgets. And mounted on his head was something that could only be described as a high-tech football helmet. Wires and lights covered the helmet like electronic ivy, and the whole lot of it was connected to a tiny radar dish sticking out of the top of it.

The plum spotted Larryboy, broke loose from the policemen, and ran up to the superhero.

"Larryboy, you've got to help me, doncha know?" the plum begged. "I'm Officer Olaf, but somehow my body has been changed into this...this...*plum!*"

"You can't be Officer Olaf," said Larryboy. "I just saw him a few minutes ago."

"Don't I sound like Olaf?"

"You're a good impersonator. Can you do the president?"

"Okay, I'll *prove* that I'm Officer Olaf!" the plum told Larryboy. "I'll tell you something that only you and I could know!"

But the plum never got a chance to prove himself. At

that very moment, a twister came roaring around the corner, hungry for destruction. It sucked up cars and spit out the engines like prune pits. It shattered windows and uprooted trees.

And in its path was the Larrymobile...

Sensing danger, Fred the Computer started the engine and squealed out of the parking space—without anyone behind the steering wheel.

"Hey, wait for me!" Larryboy shouted, running after his car, which clearly had a mind of its own.

But so did the tornado. It knew exactly where it was going as it swirled straight for the plum. Larryboy watched in horror as the tornado bore down on the poor plum, sucked him into the wild whirlwind, and then tore off down the street.

CHAPTER 4

IF I ONLY HAD A HEART...
7:45 A.M

Larryboy leaped into the Larrymobile.

"Follow that twister!" Larryboy yelled, as he put the car into gear. But the Larrymobile's engine sputtered and stalled.

"We're out of gas," said Fred. "Peanut brittle! I was really looking forward to chasing that tornado."

"We can't be out of gas!" Larryboy shouted. "Archie filled the tank this morning."

"And look! The engine is overheated," said Fred. Steam billowed from under the hood of the Larrymobile.

"I know what you're doing, Fred! You're trying to get out of chasing that tornado!"

"Now why would I want to avoid chasing a storm that is the most dangerous kind in nature? Whoops! Is that a tire I hear falling off?"

One of the plunger tires on the Larrymobile popped off and wobbled down the street.

In frustration, Larryboy clunked his head down on the steering wheel, causing an air bag to discharge in his face.

"Oops," said Fred. "My mistake."

Meanwhile, the terrifying twister roared through Bumblyburg, passed Bumbly Park, and left the city. It was headed straight for a tiny farmhouse in the middle of nowhere. But instead of flattening the house, it stopped on a spot right next to the barn. The ground opened up below the twister and the storm disappeared into the earth.

The twister dropped into a large, underground room and shut down its power. The black, twisting cloud vanished like a genie in a bottle. All that was left was a small, round vehicle, which had been spinning at the very center of the tornado. As it slowly came to a stop, a hatch popped open with a *hisssssss*.

Out stepped a plum...the very same plum who had been sucked up by the tornado just moments before. But this was no ordinary plum. He was diabolical. He was sinister. He was—

"Now wasn't that a funsy-wunsy ride?" the plum asked his Teddy Bear.

He was a plum that liked stuffed animals. But that didn't make him warm and fuzzy. *No sir!* This was one mean, old plum. His name: Plum Loco.

"Those fools have no idea that I switched brains with Officer Olaf and put my brain in his body," Plum Loco giggled to his Teddy Bear, one of a hundred stuffed animals cluttering up his secret laboratory. "And it was so *easy!* What a perfect way to steal stuffed animals!"

It was true. Plum Loco had used his twisted twister machine to switch brains with Officer Olaf. Plum Loco's brain wound up inside Officer Olaf's body, while Olaf's brain wound up in the plum's body. After pulling off the toy-store robbery, Plum Loco had reversed the process.

Their brains were back to normal—although Plum Loco wasn't someone who could really be referred to as normal.

On the wall in front of this plum was the giant map of a brain, spread out like a huge map of the world. The Veggie brain *was* Plum Loco's world. He was a brain surgeon gone bad.

Plum Loco thrived on being mean to others. He didn't have a heart, and he didn't care. In fact, he was sick of hearts. On Valentine's Day, he bought his chocolates in a brain-shaped box, rather than a heart-shaped box. His bumper sticker said, "Brains R Us."

He had even changed the titles of famous songs to:

"I Left My Brain in San Francisco."

"Put a Little Love in Your Brain."

"Achy Breaky Brain."

Plum Loco laughed, "Switching brains with Officer Olaf was only the beginning of Operation Unkind. I've got many more stuffed animals to pilfer and lots more Veggies to pick on. The question is, who's next?"

Plum Loco bent down and whispered into the ear of his Teddy Bear. "Perhaps I'll even switch brains with a superhero."

This guy had one twisted mind.

CHAPTER 5

TOO COOL FOR KINDNESS
10:30 A.M.

Tornadoes weren't the only force of nature in Bumblyburg.

At the *Daily Bumble* newspaper, other powers were on the loose. Their names were Ziggy Pickle and Ricky Avocado—two paperboys who thought they were too cool for words. Ziggy and Ricky were strong, good-looking, and popular. But they were also as unpredictable as twisters. Kindness was not their trademark.

Junior Asparagus, cub reporter for the *Daily Bumble*, tried to stay out of their way. Little did Junior know that, by some strange twist of fortune, today their paths would cross in a most unusual way.

It all started with stares. As Junior moved through the halls of the *Daily Bumble*, people kept turning and looking at him with puzzled expressions. And when he strolled by the circulation department, several paperboys and papergirls laughed and pointed. In fact, about the only papergirl who didn't snicker was his friend, Laura.

"Hey Junior!" called Laura Carrot, hopping up to him.

"What's with the hanger?"

"The what?"

"The clothes hanger," chuckled Laura. "There's a hanger sticking out the back of your shirt."

Junior craned his neck around. Sure enough, a clothes hanger was sticking out of his shirt. How humiliating! No wonder everyone was staring!

"I dressed kinda fast this morning and forgot to take it out," Junior said, blushing.

Junior decided he had better pull out the hanger as fast as he could, before anyone else saw him. But something made him pause. Two shadows passed over him like storm clouds. Slowly, he looked up and found himself staring into the dark eyes of Ziggy and Ricky.

His heart sank. This had to be the worst possible timing. Ziggy and Ricky were going to tease him for the rest of the year for showing up with a clothes hanger in his shirt. Junior felt like crawling into a hole.

But that didn't happen. Ziggy and Ricky stared at Junior for the longest, most awful minute. Finally, they spoke.

"Hey, that's actually pretty cool, Junior," said Ziggy.

"That's *way* cool," added Ricky. "Did you come up with the idea yourself?"

"Well...uh...Actually, I did."

Wow! Junior thought. *Do these guys really mean it? Do they actually think I'm cool because I'm wearing a clothes hanger in my shirt?*

"That's the coolest idea I've seen all year!" Ziggy beamed, stepping up beside Junior.

And then they spoke the words he never thought he would hear...

"Hey, Junior, want to help us with our paper route today?"

Helping them deliver papers was one of the highest honors around. But Junior played it cool and tried not to look too excited.

"Sure, why not," he answered, jumping up and down and screaming for joy inside.

Laura wasn't nearly as excited. She didn't like the sound of this. It was as if warning sirens were going off in her brain like the ones alerting all of Bumblyburg to the stormy weather.

CHAPTER 6

BRAINSTORMS

11:00 A.M.

"It's a new style. I'm starting a fad," Junior told Larry the Janitor, as he entered the meeting room of the *Daily Bumble*. The clothes hanger was still sticking out of the back of his shirt.

"No kidding," said Larry. "That's pretty cool. Where can I get one of those?"

"Try a closet. They're called hangers," said Bob the Tomato, carrying a stack of papers into the room for the daily staff meeting.

"It's very bold," Larry said. "It really makes a statement."

"I'll give you a statement," Bob scowled. "Get back to work."

"Right away, Chief!" Larry said, as he hopped to it.

Larry the Janitor dusted in the background, while the staff talked news. It was their daily brainstorming session.

Little did the staff know that Larry, the mild-mannered janitor, was also the caped cucumber. He was the purple, plunger-headed defender of all that is good, true, and in need of vacuuming. He was...*Larryboy!*

"All right," said Bob, the top tomato at the newspaper. "What do we have for the front page, besides two stories on the tornadoes?"

"Plum Loco, the famous brain surgeon, is in town giving a lecture," said Vicki Cucumber, flipping through her notes.

"Sounds interesting," said Larry, dusting Bob's head.

"Larry, my head does *not* need dusting!" Bob shouted.

"Sorry." Larry started dusting Bob's coffee mug.

"We're trying to have a meeting here," said Bob. "Why don't you forget the dusting for now?"

"Sure thing, Chief."

Larry pulled out his vacuum cleaner—his trusty Cyclone 1000.

"So what do we have on the robbery at Mr. Snappy's Extremely Gigantic Toy Emporium?" asked Bob. "I heard that all of the stuffed animals were stolen."

Larry's heart leaped into his throat. (Not literally. That would be too gross. It's just an expression.) He was shocked.

"All of the stuffed animals were stolen?" Larry said. "Then Officer Olaf was right!"

"What do you mean?" asked Vicki.

"A friend of mine saw Officer Olaf putting stuffed animals into an armored car for protection this morning," said Larry. "Somebody must have stolen them from the armored car!"

"But Mr. Snappy said the toys were stolen right out of his store," Bob clarified, very surprised. "He didn't say anything about giving them to Officer Olaf to protect!"

Larry turned on his vacuum cleaner and began to push it around the room.

"Vicki, you'd better check on this story about Officer

Olaf," Bob shouted over the noise of the vaccuum. "And turn that thing off, Larry! We're trying to talk!"

"Sure thing, Chief."

Unfortunately, Larry didn't push the Off button. By mistake, he pushed the button for supersuction cyclone.

ROOOOAAAARRRRRR!

The supersuction vacuum came alive and sucked up the drapes that Larry had been vacuuming. **THOOOOOMP!**

It was like a wild animal, devouring things right and left.

"LARRY, TURN THAT THING OFF!"

"I'M TRYING!"

But it was too late. The Cyclone 1000 vacuum cleaner went on a rampage.

It sucked up all of Bob's papers from the table.

It swallowed an entire mug of coffee.

It chased two reporters around the conference table.

It sucked all of the water out of the water cooler.

It even latched onto Bob's nose.

In fact, the Cyclone 1000 might have swallowed Bob the Tomato whole if Larry hadn't finally remembered another way to stop the machine—he pulled out the plug.

Silence fell over the staff. The meeting room was in shambles.

"The commercial was right. This vacuum sure has super-suction power," said Larry.

At that moment, a piece of the ceiling crumbled and fell right on top of Bob. Larry hurried over and dusted the debris off of Bob's head.

"I guess you needed dusting after all," Larry said.

Bob wasn't smiling.

CHAPTER 7

AN EMERGENCY WEATHER BULLETIN
11:32 A.M.

We interrupt this story with an emergency weather bulletin.

A cool front has been seen moving through the halls of the *Daily Bumble* newspaper. This cool front, made up of several cool kids, is expected to move in from the west. The cool kids are heading toward warm, kind-hearted kids, creating a dangerous, unstable situation.

If you are anywhere near these cool kids, please find shelter immediately. We repeat. Please find shelter immediately.

We now return you to your regularly scheduled story...

CHAPTER 8

BULLY BOWLING
11:33 A.M.

Junior Asparagus strutted through the halls of the *Daily Bumble*, with Ricky on one side and Ziggy on the other. He felt like a king. Ricky and Ziggy were wearing hangers in their shirts, too.

A new style had been born.

The old disco song, "Staying Aloof," blared with every step they took. (Ziggy and Ricky always played that song on a boom box whenever they strutted down the hall.)

"000-000-000-000, STAYING ALOOF, STAYING ALOOF. 000-000-000-000, STAYING ALOOOOOOF!"

The three sang at the top of their lungs.

Paperboys and girls stared at them every step of the way. Only this time there were no snickers. If Ricky and Ziggy wore hangers, it *had* to be cool.

The trio made quite a team—Ziggy, Ricky, and Junior.

"Oh my," cooed a papergirl as they passed by and looked her direction.

Things were going great for Junior—until the triumphant trio came upon two of Junior's

39

friends. Wally and Herbert were paperboys too and definitely *not* cool in the eyes of Ziggy and Ricky.

"Hey, let's have some fun," snickered Ziggy.

"I'm up for it," Ricky agreed.

"Let's not," squeaked Junior, but the two bullies weren't listening.

"Time to go bowling," Ziggy said.

Just what Junior was afraid of. You see, Ziggy and Ricky liked to bowl. But not the kind of bowling you're thinking of. When Ziggy and Ricky went bowling, they bowled Veggies over. They sent bowling balls zipping down hallways and sidewalks, knocking over broccoli, zucchinis, and carrots like bowling pins. You might say they were equal opportunity bowlers, and literally no one who got in the way stood a chance.

"I'm not really in the mood for bowling. What about soccer?" Junior asked, as Ziggy pulled his bowling ball out of his backpack. Ziggy never went anywhere without it.

"Nah, soccer's no fun."

"Then how about if we go get our paychecks?" Junior suggested.

"My money's not going anywhere," Ziggy said, lining up his shot.

Taking three bounces forward, Ziggy let loose. The bowling ball zoomed down the hall. His precision was amazing. Ziggy's ball hit Wally, knocking him into Herbert, and both of them crashed to the floor.

"Great shot!" shouted Ricky.

Herbert glanced up, his goofy sunglasses shattered. "Oh hi, Junior," he said, with a weak smile. "Nice hanger."

Junior didn't know what to say.

But he did know what to do. Junior knew God would want him to be kind. He knew he should help Wally and Herbert get back up. But if he did that, Ricky and Ziggy would turn on *him*.

"Are you friends with these two guys?" Ziggy asked Junior with a scowl.

Junior looked at Wally. Then at Herbert. Then he stared into the accusing eyes of Ziggy and Ricky.

"Ahh, not really," Junior said quietly.

"Good answer," Ziggy told him.

The trio continued to strut through the circulation department like kings...but Junior no longer felt like a king. A traitor was more like it.

"OOO-OOO-OOO-OOO, STAYING ALOOF, STAYING ALOOF! OOO-OOO-OOO-OOO, STAYING ALOOOOOOF!"

CHAPTER 9
THE MASKED TAILOR!
12:01 P.M.

Meanwhile, our plunger-headed hero headed to his Superhero 101 class, which was usually held at the Bumblyburg Community College.

But today was special. Their teacher, Bok Choy, took them on a field trip to the Masked-Tailor Superhero Costume Factory, secretly hidden deep below an ordinary clothes store.

Most members of the superhero class were there—Lemon Twist, Iron Clad, Electro-Melon, Bubble Gum, Scarlet Tomato, and others. All of these heroes had their costumes made at the factory. But the factory had never been set up for superhero tours...until now.

"I am the Masked Tailor. Welcome to our factory," said the owner, a masked string bean dressed in black. He wore the latest in capes—a high-tech cloak that could even flap indoors without wind.

The tour was amazing. Bok Choy's superhero class got to see where the Superseamstresses (all wearing masks) sewed the costumes. They wandered through a museum that told the longtime history of superhero costumes. (The very first costumes were made out of rock, which explained why prehistoric superheroes couldn't fly more than a foot off the ground.)

After the "Salute to Spandex" musical show in the factory auditorium, the superheroes even got a chance to improve their costume-changing skills. A special simulation center had been set up with hundreds of telephone booths. Each superhero was timed on how fast he or she could change into their costumes and then emerge from the phone booths.

The class concluded in what looked like an ordinary classroom.

"I'd like to end this field trip with a one-question, extra-credit quiz," announced Bok Choy. "My question is this: what is the most important thing that a superhero should wear?"

The superheroes gave the usual answers: mask, cape, utility belt, emblem, magnetic undershirt, atomic-powered slippers.

But they were all wrong.

"For the answer, turn to Section 51, Paragraph 3, Line 12 in your *Superhero Handbook*," said Bok Choy.

The Scarlet Tomato read it aloud: "You are God's chosen people. You are holy and dearly loved. So put on tender mercy and kindness as if they were your clothes."

"None of our superpowers or supercostumes would be any good if we didn't clothe ourselves with kindness," said Bok Choy. "That way, when people look at us, they see our kindness—just as clearly as they see our superhero costumes. Remember: superheroes have a heart."

No sooner had he said this than the lights in the class-room began to flicker. Weather-warning sirens began wailing. The Masked Tailor threw open the door and shouted, "A twister is heading straight for the store upstairs! You've got to help!"

The superheroes reacted with blazing speed. Scrambling out of the room, they barged up a spiral stair-case that led directly to the Vegetable Bin clothing store above. What the superheroes saw was truly shocking.

Whirling right in front of the store was another torna-do. But strangely enough, the twister simply spun in place—like some giant, deadly top.

"Let me handle this!" Lemon Twist shouted. "This job is right up my alley."

Right up her tornado alley, that is. Lemon Twist had the amazing ability to control wind within a one-foot radius of her body. She was the perfect match for the twister roaring outside the door.

Lemon Twist went whirling outside. And that's when the twister made its move. It rushed forward like a pounc-ing beast. When the twister smashed into Lemon Twist, the force of wind increased seven times over.

The roof of the clothing store ripped right off the top of it. Hundreds of clothing items went flying out of the top of the building like birds. The twister swallowed up Lemon Twist, and then it turned and whirled away, leaving may-hem in its trail.

CHAPTER 10

THE HEART OF DARKNESS
2:03 P.M.

The famous brain surgeon Plum Loco once again showed up at the police station. Only this time he claimed to be the superhero Lemon Twist. Stranger yet, the real Lemon Twist was spotted on the east side of town STEALING STUFFED ANIMALS out of the homes of Veggie children!

Larryboy was stunned.

"I can't believe that Lemon Twist would rob anyone," he told Archie back at the Larrycave.

"It's certainly odd," agreed Archie. "But here's something even stranger. The tornadoes cropping up around Bumblyburg don't appear to be naturally occurring. I think that they may have been artificially created by something evil."

Larryboy took a big gulp of his chocolate malt, leaving a chocolate mustache on his upper lip.

"If that's the case, then we should be able to turn these twisters off! But how?"

"There's only one way to find out."

"And what's that?" asked Larryboy.

Archie paused dramatically. "Someone must get into the very center of this mysterious whirlwind by flying into the tornado."

"Wow! But who would be crazy enough to fly into the middle of a twister?" Larryboy asked.

Archie continued to stare at Larryboy, as if to answer his question.

Larryboy glanced behind himself, hoping somebody else was standing there. There wasn't.

"Peanut brittle," said Larryboy. "You're looking at me, aren't you?"

Fifteen minutes later, he was soaring high over Bumblyburg in the Larryplane.

"This is crazy!" Larryboy said.

The caped cucumber couldn't believe that Archie had talked him into flying his plane right into a swirling mass of killer wind. He also couldn't believe the other problem that he had to deal with—Fred the Computer.

"Land this plane! **PLEEEEEEEEEASE!**" pleaded Fred. "I'm afraid of heights!"

"You're a computer, Fred. How can you be afraid of heights?"

"I don't know! How can computers run the Internet? It's all a mystery to me!"

"Why didn't you tell Archie you were afraid of heights?"

"Archie installed me in the Larrymobile. How was I supposed to know that your car changed into an airplane?"

Larryboy dove low over the city.

"WHOOOOOOOOOOAAA!" screamed Fred. "I'm going to be sick!"

"Twister dead ahead!" Larryboy shouted.

"Do you have to say the word *dead?* I can't look. I'm keeping my eyes closed."

"You're a computer. You don't have eyes."

The Larryplane closed in on the twister, which swirled just outside the city.

"My ears are popping!" shouted Fred. "My ears are popping!"

"You're a computer. You don't have ears."

The tornado appeared to be heading straight for a farmhouse. The Larryplane picked up speed.

"Remind me why we are about to fly into a tornado," Fred begged him, increasingly panicked.

"We're going to try to turn off this twister. But don't worry, Fred. Archie made some changes to the plane so it can survive two-hundred-mile-per-hour, twisting winds."

"But how do you know his changes will work? Archie isn't perfect! He made *me*, didn't he?"

Larryboy had to admit that Fred had a good point. But there was no turning back now. The Larryplane zoomed straight into the side of the monstrous storm, and the funnel cloud swallowed the little plane like a giant fly.

CHAPTER 11

A MOOOO-VING EXPERIENCE
2:55 P.M.

Larryboy couldn't believe it. He was looking at one of the greatest mysteries of nature—the inside of a tornado. The Larryplane spun around and around and around and around and around and around and...Now add about three hundred million more *arounds*, all in about ten minutes. That's how fast the twister spun the plane.

By this time, Fred had completely blacked out. (Of course, computers can't black out, but leave it to Fred to find a way.)

Inside the vortex of the tornado, all sorts of things whirled around, along with the Larryplane.

Pieces of wood.

A rocking chair.

Ma Mushroom riding a bicycle.

Two penguins playing checkers.

An air compressor.

A flying monkey.

An oil tanker.

And three cows.

At the state fair every year, Larryboy's

favorite ride was the Nauseator, which spun him at speeds that would tie his stomach in knots for days. But that was nothing compared to this twister.

Suddenly, the wind whipped the cockpit hatch off of the plane, leaving Larryboy completely exposed to the storm. He ducked as a piece of wood zipped by him, just inches above his head.

"That was close. Good thing I've got catlike reflexes. Otherwise, I might have—"

WHAP!

Larryboy forgot about the funnel effect—what goes around comes around. The piece of wood got him on the next lap around.

When Larryboy regained consciousness, he was lying in a haystack. His airplane was sticking through the side of a barn, and Fred was calling for a medic.

Very woozy and sore, Larryboy got up on his wobbly feet.

Feet?

Larryboy looked down. He not only had feet. He had *four* of them!

Running to a nearby farm pond, Larryboy stared at his reflection in the water. He couldn't believe what he saw.

HE WAS A COW!

How in the world did his brain wind up in the body of a cow? Was it all a bad dream? Was it from hitting his head? Had he landed somewhere over the rainbow?

Then somebody behind him said, **"MOOO."**

Larryboy whirled around and fell over. (It's not so easy to whirl on four feet.) He couldn't believe what he saw. He

saw himself wandering around nibbling on grass. Or at
least he saw someone who *looked* just like him wandering around nibbling on grass.

Larryboy, the cow, ambled over to the other Larryboy.

"Who are you?" he asked. "Are you me? Or am I you?"

The other Larryboy swallowed a mouthful of grass.
Then he simply smacked his lips and said, **"MOOOOOO."**

This was unbelievable. Larryboy's brain had been
switched with the brain of a cow!

CHAPTER 12

AN EMERGENCY WEATHER BULLETIN
3:29 P.M.

We interrupt this story with an emergency weather bulletin.

A cool-kid warning remains in effect for the rest of our book. These cool kids strike like lightning and pack heavy winds. Be ready to seek shelter at a moment's notice.

The National Weather Service has also issued a kindness watch, which means conditions are right for acts of kindness to occur. In fact, there is a thirty percent chance of lightly scattered kindness.

So keep your eyes open.

We now return you to your regularly scheduled story...

CHAPTER 13

BOWLED OVER
3:30 P.M.

It's amazing how quickly a fad can spread. By afternoon, a bunch of kids at Bumbly Park were strutting their stuff with clothes hangers in their shirts.

Meanwhile, Junior left the *Daily Bumble* and cut through the park on his bicycle. He spotted Ricky and Ziggy, who were loaded down with the afternoon edition of the newspaper.

"I'm here to help you deliver papers," Junior beamed. Hanging with Ziggy and Ricky brought with it amazing prestige. *Wait till my friends see this!* he thought.

"Great!" said Ziggy. "Maybe you can go bowling with us when we're done."

"Really? I'd love to!" he replied. But then it hit him. Ziggy wasn't talking about the kind of bowling most people do. Ziggy meant bully-bowling.

Junior's heart sank. "Ummm...I don't know if I can."

Ziggy's eyes became dark and narrowed.

"Listen, Asparagus. You're one of us now. And

57

that doesn't happen to many Veggies. You'd better go bowling with us...or else."

Being cool suddenly didn't seem all that hot. Junior gulped. "Who...who are you planning to bowl over?"

"Who else?" laughed Ziggy. "Those two losers over there."

Junior looked down the sidewalk. Ziggy was talking about Wally and Herbert, who were both loaded down with their own newspapers to deliver.

"But you've already bowled them over today."

"We're trying for a turkey...that means we've got two strikes to go!" said Ricky.

"We'll do the actual bowling. All you have to do is retrieve our bowling balls when we're done," Ziggy told him. "Whataya say, kid?"

This was Junior's big chance to take a stand. But which stand would he take? To be cool like Ziggy and Ricky? Or stand up for what's right and show kindness?

"We're waiting for an answer, Asparagus," growled Ziggy.

Junior didn't know what to do.

"Come on, Asparagus. Be cool and rule. Or be a loser and drool."

"Either way, you're part of the game," snickered Ziggy. "You can help us, or we're going to bowl *you* over. Take your pick."

Junior looked around. A group of kids had collected and were hanging on every word. He took one last look at Ziggy's ugly stare. He was scared.

"Let's go bowling," he muttered.

CHAPTER 14

COW-BOY
3:32 P.M.

Meanwhile, we last left Larryboy in the body of a cow, while Fred the Computer called for a medic.

"I'm melting, I'm melting!" shouted Fred.

Larryboy ran over to the crashed Larryplane, which was still sticking out of the side of the barn.

"Do something!" Fred said. "Call an ambulance! Call a programmer!"

"You're a computer, Fred. You don't need an ambulance."

"I've already lost two pints of data," said Fred, freaking out. "I'm going to need a transfusion from a laptop. Hurry! I'm moving toward the bright light!"

Suddenly, the computer went quiet for a few moments—very unusual for Fred. "Hey, you're not Larryboy. You're a talking cow," he said.

"No, I'm Larryboy. That twister put my brain in the body of a cow."

Stunned silence. Then Fred started giggling. Pretty soon, the computer couldn't control himself.

"Say, Larryboy, did you hear this one? What do you call it when super cows do battle? Steer Wars!"

Larryboy was not amused.

"And where does Superman's cow live? In Moo-tropolis!"

"Very funny, Fred."

"Hey, don't have a cow, man! Or should I say, don't have a man, cow?" Fred couldn't stop laughing.

While Fred continued with his antics, Larryboy used one of his hooves to push the communicator button in the plane's cockpit. Archie popped up on the high-definition video monitor.

"Larryboy, are you behind that cow?" asked Archie. "Larryboy! Come in! A cow seems to have triggered the videophone."

"Bad news, Archie. I *am* the cow. My brain is in this cow's body."

There was a long pause on the other end of the videophone. Archie blinked in shock. "Okay, don't panic. Don't panic. We can still do this."

"How?" asked Larryboy.

"How now brown cow?" snickered Fred.

"Listen closely," Archie ordered. "There's a spare pair of supersuction ears in the back of the Larryplane. I think they'll fit over the ears on your cow head."

"What do you call a hero who gets superpowers after being bitten by a radioactive cow?" asked Fred. "A moootant!"

"There's also a minicomputer under the front seat—a computer so small you can carry it like a portable CD player," said Archie. "Plug it into the airplane's controls and download Fred onto it. That way, you'll have Fred with you for help."

"What sound effect does Bat-Cow make when he fights villains?" giggled Fred. **"COW-POW!"**

"I'm not sure that I really want Fred with me."

"Of course you do. Without him, I don't see how you'd be able to track down Plum Loco. I'm convinced that he's behind all of this."

"But Fred is awfully emotional," said Larryboy. "One second he's getting mad. Then he's panicking. Now he can't stop laughing."

"I'm e-moooooo-tional," laughed Fred.

"I programmed emotions into Fred so that he'd be a computer with a heart. Remember your superhero lesson? Heroes have a heart. But perhaps I overdid the emotion programming."

"I'm e-mooooooooo-tional," Fred chuckled again.

"Oh dear," Larryboy sighed, but he did exactly as Archie asked. He slipped a pair of supersuction ears over his cow ears, downloaded Fred onto the minicomputer, and attached the computer to the cowbell hanging around his neck.

"Look at me! I'm a cowbell!" shouted Fred. "Of course, I'd rather be a cow-*boy*, but I suppose this will have to do."

As for Larryboy, he stood in the farm field with a purple mask on his face, supersuction plunger ears over his cow-ears, and a minicomputer around his neck.

The fate of Bumblyburg rested in the hands of a cow.

CHAPTER 15

BRAIN-TWISTER 2
3:44 P.M.

Larryboy had to
admit that Fred came in handy.
Within three minutes, Fred had figured
out that there was a secret headquarters
underground—right beneath their feet.

And a minute after that, Fred figured out that
you could enter the secret headquarters through the
farmhouse's storm-cellar doors.

And two minutes after *that*, he came up with the
password to get them inside the cellar.

And ten seconds after *that*...Larryboy tumbled head
over hooves down the cellar stairs.

"You're an *udder* failure when it comes to going
down stairs," chuckled Fred.

"I don't think I'll ever wish I had feet again," muttered Larryboy.

The first room they entered in the underground
headquarters was filled with pictures and diagrams of
brains. A giant, clear-plastic model of a brain stood in
the center of the room. But there was no sign of life.

The song, "Don't Go Breaking My Brain,"
played over an intercom.

"Hook me up to one of those computers

on the wall," said Fred.

"Sure thing."

One minute later, Fred was sifting through all of the information on Plum Loco's computer system.

"Archie is right," Fred calculated. "Plum Loco is the guy who's been switching brains around. His invention is called the Brain-Twister—a tornado that switches brains between different bodies. Amazing."

But suddenly, Fred started crying. It began with quiet weeping. But then he cut loose with some heavy sobs.

"Now what, Fred? You're a computer," Larryboy told him. "You can't cry."

"It's my disk drive, and I'll cry if I want to," sobbed Fred. "I've just tapped into Plum Loco's diary...and...and..."

"What is it, Fred?"

"It seems as though Plum Loco never had any friends growing up. Other kids teased him and called him a brainiac. Nerd. Geek. Four eyes. It's all so sad...I...I..."

"Get a hold of yourself, Fred."

"Plum Loco never received a single birthday present when he was growing up."

"Never?" asked Larryboy. "So that explains his dastardly deeds."

"Yes, it does. Plum Loco decided to use his massive brainpower to devise mean tricks. And get this. Today is his birthday, which probably explains the reason for his attack. It's all so sad..."

"Is Plum Loco the one who's been stealing all the stuffed animals?" asked Larryboy.

"That's right."

"But why?"

"It seems that Plum Loco surrounded himself with stuffed animals while he was growing up. Since no one was ever kind to him, he had to turn to stuffed animals, the next best thing. He could never get enough. They were warm. They were fuzzy. Since then, his plan has been to take every stuffed animal in the world."

Fred was boo-hooing now.

"Control yourself or you're going to blow your circuits," said Larryboy. "Besides, we've got to be quiet."

Larryboy crept silently into the next room—as quiet as one could with four cow hooves and a bell. He heard someone talking.

Peering out from behind a stack of gadgets and blinking contraptions, Larryboy spotted Plum Loco. The mad scientist was in the middle of the room, fiddling with the controls of a newer, larger Brain-Twister. The round ship hovered three feet above the ground.

"Switching brains with a superhero like Lemon Twist was so much fun," Plum Loco told his Teddy Bear. "But the citizens of Bumblyburg haven't seen anything yet. My first Brain-Twister was a toy compared to the Brain-Twister 2. I'll be able to switch the brains of *hundreds* of people all at the same time! And then I'll get my final revenge by destroying the entire city of Bumblyburg!"

"You'd better do something fast," Fred whispered to Larryboy. "Notice I said the word *you*."

Fred was right. It was time for this cow to become an action hero.

CHAPTER 16

THE BIG SWITCHEROO
4:04 P.M.

"Cowabunga, baby!" shouted Larryboy as he leaped out from his hiding place. He tried a "cow fu" stance, but that wasn't easy with four cow legs. Larryboy wound up flat on his tail.

Plum Loco spun around in surprise. Then he laughed, threw open the hatch on the top of the Brain-Twister 2, and hopped inside. "I'll get you, my pretty, and your little computer, too!" he cackled.

As the Brain-Twister 2 fired up its power, Larryboy turned his cow head and fired a supersuction plunger ear. The plunger tore across the room and stuck fast to the side of the ship. **THONK!**

"Now what?" asked Fred.

"I haven't thought that far ahead," said Larryboy.

"Big mistake."

Fred was right.

The Brain-Twister 2 rose high in the air until it hovered midway between the floor and the ceiling. And then it began to spin. Slowly at first. Then it built up speed and power.

Since Larryboy (and Fred) were connected to the ship

by the plunger cord, they, too, began to spin. Faster and faster and faster and faster.

"AHHHHHHHHHHHHHHHHHHHHHHHHHH!" Larryboy yelled.
"AHHHHHHHHHHHHHHHHHHHHHHHHHH!" Fred yelled.

The Brain-Twister 2 began spinning at speeds that would make an astronaut sick to his stomach. As it twirled, the ship created a powerful, spinning wind. It had become a twister! Directly above the twister, the ground opened up. If anyone had been watching, it would have appeared as if the very earth itself had opened its mouth.

Come to think of it, there *was* someone watching above ground. The cow—actually the cow in Larryboy's body. Despite the fact that he was busy munching on grass, this spectacle caused even him to be curious. So this cow (who looked like Larryboy) wandered over to the big hole that had just opened up in the ground. He peered inside.

"MOOOOOO?"

The twister rose out of the ground. Within an instant, the tornado had sucked up the cow that looked like Larryboy along with every other chicken and pig that it passed over as it cut across the farmland.

Then as it turned and headed for the city, the tornado began hurling animals out of its funnel cloud—just as fast as it was sucking them up. It looked like it was raining pigs and chickens.

"OOF!"
"MOO!"
"OUCH!"
"OINK!"

That was the sound of Larryboy, Fred, the cow, and a

pig being spit out of the twister and hitting the ground. But the million-dollar question was, when they landed, who had whose brain?

The good news was that Larryboy's brain was no longer inside that cow. A pig's brain was inside the poor creature instead.

The bad news was that Larryboy's brain did not wind up back inside his own body. His brain ended up inside the portable minicomputer, where Fred had been stored.

Hmmmmmm...Then what happened to Fred the Computer?

His computer brain wound up inside Larryboy's body.

Fred looked down at his brand-new, cucumber body and said, "Larryboy, I don't think we're in Kansas anymore."

CHAPTER 17

CLOUDY, WITH A CHANCE OF KINDNESS
4:05 P.M.

Meanwhile, back at Bumbly Park, Ziggy and Ricky had bowled perfect strikes. Ziggy's bowling ball sent Wally hurtling into the bushes, while Ricky's hook shot knocked Herbert ten feet into the air. Their newspapers went flying in all directions.

Junior felt horrible as he watched Wally and Herbert struggle to get up and then run around trying to catch their papers before they blew away. Lots of other kids stood around watching, too. Only Laura Carrot had the courage—and the heart—to help them.

"Gee thanks, Laura," said Wally.

"Yeah, you're a pal," added Herbert. "What's gotten into Junior today?"

"He's too cool to care," muttered Laura, her anger rising.

Meanwhile, Ziggy and Ricky prepared for another frame of bully bowling.

"Who do you want to take out this time?" Ziggy asked Ricky.

"I'll take Wally *and* the carrot girl. It's a tricky shot, but I love a challenge."

73

"But you already got your turkey!" Junior exclaimed.

"Chill out, Asparagus. We've got a perfect game going. Can't stop now."

"Wait till they pick up all of their papers," Ricky snickered. "Then we'll roll again."

Junior didn't know what to say. He looked at all of the kids standing around, just watching. No one wanted to help. No one showed an ounce of kindness—except for Laura.

"This isn't who I want to be," Junior found himself saying. "I quit."

"You what?" asked Ricky.

"Don't have the guts to bowl with the big boys?" Ziggy smirked.

"This isn't my kind of game," Junior told them. "Someday you just might wind up in Wally and Herbert's shoes, and you won't like it either!"

"They don't *wear* shoes, Asparagus boy!" Ricky chuckled.

"Besides, that'll never happen," Ziggy told him. "There's no way we'd ever be caught wearing anything they would wear."

"And *I'm* no longer going to be caught wearing *this* silly thing in *my* clothes!" Junior said. Then he yanked the hanger out from under his shirt and rushed over to help his friends pick up their papers.

"Gee thanks, Junior," smiled Herbert.

"I'm sorry I didn't do this sooner," Junior told his friends.

"We're *all* going to be sorry any second now," said Laura. "We're about to be bowled over."

Ziggy and Ricky were lining up their next shots.

"I'm not afraid of them anymore," said Junior.

"Don't sweat it, guys," said Herbert. "It looks like we've got much bigger problems than Ziggy and Ricky."

Wally, Laura, and Junior looked in the direction that Herbert was staring. Rising high above the city was a storm. It was the biggest twister they had ever seen. Its black tail scoured the ground like a snake.

And the monster was heading their way.

CHAPTER 18

TWIST AND SHOUT
4:19 P.M.

Fred couldn't have been happier.

"Look at me! I'm a cucumber! I've got a body!" Fred said as he hopped around like a little kid on Christmas morning.

"That body is just on loan," scolded Larryboy. His brain was still trapped inside the minicomputer, which still dangled from the cow's neck.

"Let's do the twist!" Fred swiveled his hips, dancing like a crazed cucumber. "Let's do the—"

"Fred..."

"Look at me! I can stand on my head!"

"*Fred...*"

"Look at me! I can do the limbo!"

"FRED! We don't have time to waste. That twister is heading straight for the heart of Bumblyburg."

Fred finally stopped jumping around and caught his breath. "Sorry, Larryboy. I got carried away."

"The entire city of Bumblyburg is going to get carried away by powerful winds if we don't do something fast!"

"But what?" asked Fred. "I can't think straight in this body. I don't know how you do it. And how do you scratch an itch in the middle of your back? It's starting to drive me crazy."

Fred paced back and forth, itching and fidgeting.

"Come to think of it, these clothes make it hard to concentrate," complained Fred. "This spandex is so tight I can hardly breathe. How do you stand it?"

Larryboy's eyes lit up. "Did you say clothes? Fred, you're a genius!"

"Can't you wear Bermuda shorts or something that allows a little more freedom of movement?" Fred asked, not paying attention to Larryboy.

"Put on tender mercy and kindness as if they were your clothes," Larryboy said, remembering the words from the *Superhero Handbook*. "It's the secret weapon that will stop Plum Loco! But we'd better act fast."

"We should?"

"Yes!"

So they did.

CHAPTER 19

MIND GAMES
4:25 P.M.

The twister hurled through
Bumblyburg with a vengeance. It
tossed billboards through the air like
giant Frisbees. It tossed garbage cans
around like toys. The storm also sucked up
fleeing Veggies like...well, kind of like
Larryboy's Cyclone 1000 vacuum cleaner. And by
the time the twister dropped the Veggies back onto
the ground, their brains had been switched.

There was complete chaos in Bumblyburg.

Baby Lou Carrot's brain had been switched with a
policeman's.

Bob the Tomato's brain wound up in Vicki
Cucumber's head.

Junior Asparagus's brain had been switched with
Laura the Carrot's.

Most amazing of all...

Wally's and Herbert's brains had been switched
with Ziggy's and Ricky's. That's right. The storm
hit Bumbly Park with amazing speed, and it did
some bowling of its own. It bowled over Wally,

Herbert, Ziggy, and Ricky, and then spit them back out about ten seconds later.

Thunderstruck, Ziggy and Ricky looked down at their new bodies. Ziggy found himself wearing a Hawaiian shirt and silly sunglasses. Ricky was wearing a turtleneck sweater and a baseball cap that was on backwards.

"AHHHHHHHHHHHHHHHHHHHHHHHHHHH!"

It was their worst nightmare.

"I want my mommy!" cried Ricky.

Meanwhile, the twister turned onto Bumbly Boulevard and set its target on downtown Bumblyburg. Plum Loco was ready for some serious revenge. He aimed to flatten every building he could find. And no one could stand in his way.

But someone *was* standing in his way. Two someones, in fact.

Larryboy and Fred.

CHAPTER 20

THE SECRET WEAPON
5:20 P.M.

Fred (still in Larryboy's body) and Larryboy
(still stuck inside the minicomputer) held their
ground. But it wasn't easy. Wind hit them like
invisible linebackers. The tornado bore down on
them, growling and rumbling and spitting lightning.

But Fred and Larryboy wouldn't budge. They stood
right beside the Larryplane, which they had been surprised to find still working. Fred had flown it to the
rescue by remote control.

"Is it time to use our secret weapon?" Fred asked.

"It's time."

Larryboy and Fred began to sing as loudly as they
could. Their voices boomed from the speaker system
built into the Larryplane.

"HAPPY BIRTHDAY TO YOU! HAPPY BIRTHDAY
TO YOU! HAPPY BIRTHDAY DEAR LOCO! HAPPY
BIRTHDAY TO YOUUUUUUUU!"

The twister slowed down—but just barely. Larryboy and Fred continued to belt
out their song, again and again.

By the time they

sang "Happy Birthday" for the fourth time, the tornado had come to a complete stop—only a short distance from our heroes. A mechanical arm shot out of the funnel cloud with a chair at the end of it. And sitting in the chair was none other than Plum Loco.

Plum Loco looked confused.

"How...how did you know that today is my birthday?" he stammered.

"I'm a computer," said Fred. "It's my job to know those things.

"Show him what we've got," said Larryboy.

Smiling, Fred reached into the cockpit of the Larryplane. He pulled out three brightly wrapped birthday presents and a delicious chocolate cake.

"For me?" gasped Plum Loco.

"Happy birthday, Loco!"

The mad scientist was stunned. No one had ever been so kind to him.

"We're sorry you never got any presents when you were growing up," said Larryboy.

"What a bummer," added Fred. "So happy birthday!"

"How did you know that I never got any presents when I was growing up?" asked the plum.

"Like I said, I'm a computer," said Fred. "It's my job to know these things."

Plum Loco had unplugged his emotions a long time ago. But somehow, some way, these three presents, the birthday cake, and the song triggered something buried deep inside him. They triggered a tiny spark of kindness.

Why else would Plum Loco do what he did next?

"I tell you what, guys," he said. "Since you scratched my back, I'll scratch yours."

"Good!" beamed Fred. "I was wondering how I was going to get that itch scratched!"

"No, I think he means he's going to do something kind for us, since we are being kind to him," pointed out Larryboy.

"What about my itch?"

"I'm going to put your brains back where they were," Plum Loco said as he pushed a button on a remote control. A tiny tornado shot from the side of the large twister and whirled straight toward Fred and Larryboy. It spun them around for a minute and then put them safely on the ground.

Their brains were back where they belonged.

"There's no place like home," said Larryboy, looking down at his cucumber body. It felt good to be back home in his very own body.

Fred didn't even mind being put back inside the mini-computer until he could be returned to his regular home. Bodies can be a lot of trouble, he decided.

"Thanks, Plummy," said Larryboy. "But can I ask one more thing?"

"Fire away, Larryboy," said the plum as he busily unwrapped the first present. It was a new lab coat, specially made for him by the Super Seamstresses at the costume factory.

"Can you turn off this twister...please? Someone could get hurt."

Plum Loco looked up sharply. Had Larryboy asked too much? Was Plum Loco's moment of kindness over?

A smile broke out on the plum's face. "Let it be my way of saying thanks."

Unfortunately, there was one big problem. Before Plum Loco could make a move to turn off the twister, the torna-do began to inch forward—without anyone steering it.

"Watch out behind you!" Larryboy warned.

"Uh-oh," said Plum Loco. "This twister is too powerful for my old braking system. It's about to—"

All at once, the twister hurled Plum Loco out of his chair and took off like a runaway train. The twister was once again headed straight for downtown Bumblyburg.

CHAPTER 21

THE IMPERFECT STORM
5:44 P.M.

Larryboy leaped into the cockpit of the Larryplane as Plum Loco stared bug-eyed at his out-of-control creation.

"Larryboy, let me go with you!" the plum shouted. "I'm the only one who knows how to turn it off!"

"Hop in, Plummy!"

The Larryplane may have been battle-bruised from the previous twister, but it could still outrun the tornado. As it raced alongside the giant twister, Larryboy fired a supersuction plunger from one of the wings.

THONK!

The plunger hit home. It zipped through the dark funnel cloud and struck the core—the heart of the twister that spun the storm. But once connected to the Brain-Twister, the Larryplane began to spin around and around and around.

"Here we go again!" shouted Fred.

"How do I turn the twister off?" Larryboy yelled over the roar.

"You have to get inside," answered Plum Loco. "Then push the red button!"

"Roger that!" Then Larryboy attempted

the impossible. As the plane spun around and around, he hooked himself onto the tether line, which extended from the plane to the center of the twister. He was going to slide down the cord and into the middle of the twister.

"Watch out for the wood this time!" Fred called out.

He was right. Pieces of wood spun around and around the funnel cloud. Larryboy had to dodge them all if he wanted to pull this off.

ZIPPPPPPPP!

Hooked to the tether, Larryboy slid down the zip line.

"Oops."

Oops was right. Just as our hero was heading for the side of the tornado, about six chunks of wood came flying around the side of the cloud.

One piece of wood skimmed his head. Two raced right by his back. One grazed his stomach. So he hopped on top of the fifth and rode it like a splintered surfboard.

"I DID IT!" Larryboy shouted before Fred could shout...

"WATCH OUT!"

Larryboy fired a supersuction ear just in time, deflecting the wood right before it slammed into his face.

Meanwhile, the tornado was closing in on the first building in its path—the Burger Bell restaurant.

The wild wind shredded two telephone poles.

Dirt spiraled into the air, blinding Larryboy.

The caped cucumber disappeared through the side of the funnel cloud.

Pieces of the Burger Bell's roof began to peel off the restaurant.

Deep inside the twister, Larryboy made his way into Plum Loco's ship.

The twister bounced a car on the ground like a basketball.

Ma Mushroom was again peddling her bike in midair.

Larryboy found the red button and pushed it.

Suddenly, the twister came to a halt. It burbled and gurgled and began to come apart. The black cloud rolled and churned...

And then it exploded. **POP! POOF!**

The tornado burst apart into millions of little, black puffy clouds.

The Larryplane was hurled backwards by the blast. It spun out of control, nose-diving toward Earth.

Fred's life flashed in front of his circuits.

Larryboy was nowhere to be seen.

CHAPTER 22

AN EMERGENCY WEATHER BULLETIN
6:06 P.M.

We interrupt the climax of this story with an emergency weather bulletin.

The National Weather Service has cancelled the Cool-Kid Warning. The storm has passed and the all-clear has sounded. Expect showers of kindness through the rest of the day.

We now return you to your regularly scheduled conclusion ...

CHAPTER 23

THE GREATEST DAY
THE NEXT DAY...

When Larryboy came to, he was in a hospital bed with a bandage on his head. He was surrounded by friendly faces—Bob the Tomato, Vicki, Archie, Lemon Twist, Bok Choy, Laura, Junior, Wally, and Herbert.

Larryboy looked around at his friends. He was groggy, but smiling.

"I had the strangest dream," Larryboy said. "And you were in it, Bob. And you were in it, Archie. And you too, Bok Choy."

"It wasn't a dream," Archie explained. "It really happened. You got quite a bump on your head."

"But you'll be glad to know that the twister has been destroyed," Laura smiled.

"When you pushed the button, it exploded," added Bob.

"And when the tornado blew up, everyone's brains were returned to them. Everybody's back to normal," said Bok Choy.

"Well, almost everybody," Junior pointed out. "Ricky and Ziggy have apologized to

Wally and Herbert. That's not exactly normal."

"And Fred...what happened to Fred?" asked Larryboy.

"I'm right here, good buddy!"

Larryboy turned his head to the left. There, lying in the hospital bed next to him, was the computer. An IV ran from the hospital's computer into Fred's side.

"The storm is over?" Larryboy asked.

"That's right," said Bob. "The sun is shining. It's a new day."

"But what about Plum Loco?" asked Larryboy. "Is he okay?"

"Just take a look to your right," said Lemon Twist.

Larryboy turned his head to the other side. There, in another hospital bed, lay the mad scientist—only he wasn't so mad anymore.

"Hello, Larryboy," said Plum Loco. "I'm sorry I switched everyone's brains, robbed the toy store, uprooted trees, and tried to destroy the city."

"You're forgiven," said Larryboy.

All at once, the door of the hospital room was flung open.

"I got here as quickly as I could, doncha know!" It was Officer Olaf. He was all smiles. He was lugging a huge load of gifts for Plum Loco, Larryboy, and Fred the Computer.

Officer Olaf pulled out a box of chocolates and handed them to Plum Loco—a box shaped like a brain. "Just the way you like it."

Right behind Olaf came Dr. Nezzer, with a big grin on his face and waving a set of X-rays. "Great news, Mr. Loco!" the doctor exclaimed. "Your X-rays are back! And they show, without a doubt, that in addition to having a great big brain, you do have a heart!"

"Thanks everyone," Plum Loco said as he looked around the room. "You're all being so kind, and I really don't deserve it."

"Nonsense!" said Bok Choy, as he stepped from behind a curtain. He pushed out a cart, which carried the largest cake any of them had ever seen.

"I think Larryboy and Fred were in the middle of celebrating someone's birthday yesterday, right before the tornado spun out of control," said Bok Choy. "There's no reason we can't finish the celebration."

So the entire group broke out into song.

"HAPPY BIRTHDAY TO YOU! HAPPY BIRTHDAY TO YOU! HAPPY BIRTHDAY DEAR LOCO! HAPPY BIRTHDAY TO YOU!"

Plum Loco leaned forward and blew out the candles.

"What did you wish for?" asked Laura.

"I didn't need to make a wish," smiled the plum, looking around. "I've already gotten what I've always wanted."

"Let's eat!" shouted Fred. "I'm starving! I want the biggest piece!"

"You can't eat cake," said Larryboy. "You're a computer."

"Then pass the computer chips."

So the party began. This really was the greatest day in Plum Loco's life. But I suppose you already figured that out.

After all, that's what you call a no-brainer.

THE END

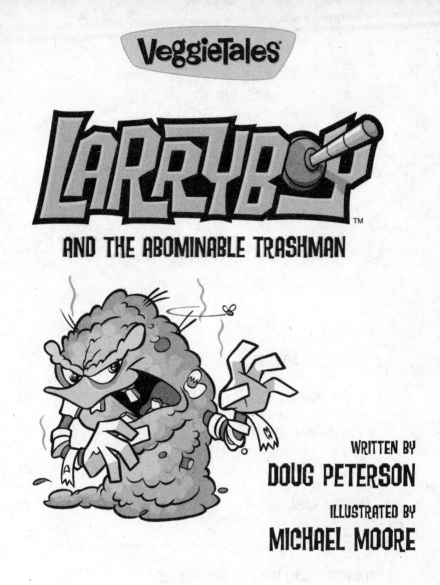

VeggieTales

LARRYBOY™

AND THE ABOMINABLE TRASHMAN

WRITTEN BY
DOUG PETERSON

ILLUSTRATED BY
MICHAEL MOORE

BASED ON THE HIT VIDEO SERIES: LARRYBOY
CREATED BY PHIL VISCHER
SERIES ADAPTED BY TOM BANCROFT

ZONDERkidz

ZONDERVAN.com/
AUTHORTRACKER
follow your favorite authors

TABLE OF CONTENTS

CHAPTER 1

CANNED MONSTER

Junior Asparagus hated taking out the trash at night—especially on a foggy night like this one. Wind whipped through the trees. Leaves spun around on the ground. The swings on the swing set were creaking in the breeze. Every sound made Junior's heart beat faster.

The Asparagus family kept *two* garbage cans out back by the garage, which were buried deep in shadow. At any moment, Junior expected something snarling to leap out at him.

"That's strange," he said, edging closer to the garbage cans. As his eyes slowly adjusted to the darkness, he could see *three* garbage cans. "I thought we had only two cans. Mom and Dad must've bought a new one," he said, as a shiver ran up his spine, did two laps around his neck, and sprinted back down.

Then it happened.

Just as Junior was about to lift the lid on the new can, the container began to move. It shook and rattled as if something was inside trying desperately to get out.

Junior dropped his garbage bag. His mouth opened wide, but he made no sound.

One heart-stopping second later, the silver lid on the new can popped off and shot eight feet into the air. That was something Junior didn't see every day. Inside the can, the garbage swirled around and around, like a whirlpool of gunk, slop, and litter. Faster and faster it spun. Then, with a roar and a **WHOOOOOSH,** the trash came together and rose up out of the can.

The garbage was *alive!*

Even stranger, the trash took on the shape of a creature. It had arms made out of discarded paper-towel tubes and Chinese take-out containers. Its head looked like it was formed out of wrinkled wrappers of all sorts. And the creature's chest was nothing but stale donuts, banana peels, and a half-eaten fish.

Even worse—the monster smelled like moldy meat, spoiled milk, and rotten eggs.

"AAAAAAHHHHHHHHHHHH!"

That was Junior screaming, in case you hadn't already guessed.

The creature rose out of the garbage can, swinging his trashy arms wildly and bellowing like a gorilla in bad need of a breath mint. The little asparagus wheeled around and dashed back to the house.

Boy, did Junior hate taking out the trash!

CHAPTER 2

EYE WITNESS

Meanwhile, at Bob the Tomato's house on the other side of Bumblyburg...

"What story do we have for the front page?" Bob said into his cordless telephone. Bob was the busy editor for the *Daily Bumble* newspaper. And like all busy editors, he was doing two things at once. He was taking out the garbage while talking on the phone.

"What!?" Bob shouted into the receiver as he bounced out the back door of his house.

"*Winklesteen Walks Dog?!* What kind of front-page story is that? If the dog had walked Winklesteen, then you'd have a story. But not *Winklesteen Walks Dog*. It's boring!"

On the other end of the phone was Vicki Cucumber, the photographer for the *Daily Bumble*.

"Sure, Phil Winklesteen was big news last month when he rescued seven puppies from Bumbly Bay," Bob said. "But since then, we've done *twenty* stories about Phil Winklesteen. Yes, I know that Phil is a big movie star. But that doesn't mean we have to report on every little thing he does!"

It was true. Phil Winklesteen *was* a big star in action movies. But Phil became more than just another movie star last month when he jumped into Bumbly Bay to rescue those poor little puppies.

He became a *real* action hero!

"I know...I know," Bob muttered into the phone. "Hey, hold on a second, Vicki."

Bob stared at his garbage cans lined up along the side of his house.

"That's odd," he said. "Somebody put a new garbage can next to my house. Yes, I'm sure it's new. I wonder where it came from."

As Bob moved closer, the garbage can began to shake.

"You aren't going to believe this," he said to Vicki over the phone. "But I think there are raccoons in my trash again."

Carefully, Bob lifted up the lid of the shiny, new can. What he saw was the last thing he ever thought he would see.

On the other end of the line, Vicki heard Bob mumble, "What in the world?" Then she heard him gasp, drop the trash-can lid, and scream.

The line went dead.

CHAPTER 3

TALES FROM THE TRASH CAN

Bumblyburg was buzzing.

The next morning, everyone was talking about the monster that had appeared all over town. The creature had leaped out of garbage cans and scared the living daylights out of everyone—including Bob the Tomato. The good news was that Bob survived his "close encounter of the trashy kind."

At the *Daily Bumble*, Bob called an emergency meeting to talk about the monster. Ten staff members crowded around the long oak table as a team of body-gourds barged through the double doors. These were buff-looking gourds in dark suits and dark sunglasses. They encircled the trash can in the *Daily Bumble* meeting room.

"Target secure," said one of the gourds

through a tiny radio. "I repeat. Target secure."

It wasn't until the gourds gave the all-clear signal that Larry the Janitor entered the meeting room—cautiously.

"I just need to empty this trash can," Larry explained to Bob as his bodygourds x-rayed the can. "With a trash monster on the loose, one can never be too careful around garbage. So don't mind us."

Bob sighed and shook his head. Then he turned to his staff and said, "So what headline do we have for today's paper?"

"What do you think of this?" Junior asked Bob. He held up the front page of the *Daily Bumble*, which said in big, bold type: **MONSTER TRASHES CITY!**

"I love it!" Bob declared, scribbling on the news story with his red pencil. "But throw on a couple more exclamation points. That monster is really scary!"

That day the entire newspaper was devoted to the mysterious monster and the twenty-seven eye-witness accounts.

"We also need a name for the monster," Bob said excitedly. "Something that'll really grab 'em."

"How about the Incredible Trash Thing?" suggested

Vicki. "People like monsters that have the word *thing* in the name."

"I like the Smelly Slop Stomper," said Lois Lemon.

The names came fast and furious.

"How about the Trash Mummy?"

"The Can-Man!"

"Can Kong!"

"The Loch Mess Monster!"

"Not bad," commented Bob.

"Gunzilla!" interjected another.

"Even better."

"How about the Abominable Trashman?"

"Who said that?" Bob shouted, bringing a sudden hush to the table.

"I did," chirped Larry the Janitor, as he sifted through the garbage can. Larry cleared his throat and continued. "You've heard of the Abominable Snowman, right? Well... this guy seems pretty abominable?"

Bob spun around in his swivel chair as he gave it some thought. Then...

"I love it!" Bob shouted, scribbling the name on a sheet of paper and handing it to an assistant. "Good work, Larry.

Now, the next thing we need to do is get a photo of the Abominable Trashman. Of all the twenty-seven places he showed up last night, we don't have a single picture to prove that he exists."

"What you need, Chief, is a stakeout," said Larry, glancing up from the trash can.

"Huh?"

"A stakeout," Larry repeated. "Somebody should watch a trash can all night and be ready with a camera."

"That's not a half-bad idea," Bob said. "Vicki, are you up for a job like that?"

"Sure thing, Chief."

Larry the Janitor stopped what he was doing to stare at Vicki. He had a goofy grin on his face and sighed deeply.

"Hey, I have an idea," Larry said after his brain finally came back to earth. "Why don't I help Vicki with the stakeout?"

"Well, I don't know...You're not a reporter or a photographer."

"But I'm a janitor! And who knows more about garbage cans than a janitor?"

"You've got a point," Bob agreed. "And the stakeout

was your idea in the first place."

So it was settled. Larry the Janitor and Vicki the Cucumber would stand guard by the Asparagus family's garbage cans at nightfall. And Larry would get a chance to spend time with Vicki—which made him quite happy.

Little did Vicki know, however, that Larry the Janitor wasn't who he appeared to be. Mild-mannered Larry was really the caped cucumber...the green guardian of Bumblyburg...the plunger-headed protector of all that is decent and good.

Larry was none other than *Larryboy!*

HE ...IS...THAT...HERO!

CHAPTER 4

MONSTER WATCH

Larry the Janitor and Vicki the Cucumber crouched behind a huge pile of garbage bags filled with leaves. It was pitch-black dark behind the Asparagus house, and the only sounds in the neighborhood were the chirping of crickets, the barking of faraway dogs—and Larry's heartbeat.

Larry was nervous. But it wasn't just the idea of a monster pouncing on him that stirred his fears. Larry was afraid that he wouldn't come up with anything good to talk about with Vicki.

"Uh...Nice night we're having," Larry said, looking around.

"Yes. Nice night," Vicki answered, fumbling for something to say.

Larry smiled awkwardly. "Uh...Did you

know that every person in the country throws away about four pounds of garbage every day?"

"No." Big pause. "I didn't." Vicki looked around. Normally, she was never at a loss for words.

"Are you afraid of the Abominable Trashman?" she finally asked, as she checked to make sure her camera was loaded with film.

"Not a bit," said Larry. "I don't have a scared bone in my body." Larry was afraid to admit that he had *several* scared bones in his body, not to mention a scared heart, scared gallbladder, scared tongue, and scared lips.

Suddenly, the crickets stopped chirping and the dogs stopped barking. A brisk wind sent a stream of leaves rushing along the ground. Branches scraped against each other, looking like skeleton arms. Something strange was happening.

"This could be it," said Larry, peeking over a bag of leaves.

They watched the three garbage cans that were not more than ten feet away. Ever so slightly, the newest of the cans started to move. Then the lid began to shake, rattle, and roll.

"Here he comes!" whispered Larry excitedly. "Are the lights set?"

Vicki nodded. They had set up floodlights and were going to flick them on the moment the monster appeared.

The entire garbage can began to shake, rattle, and rock. Vicki looked into the camera.

Everything went completely and utterly still for one-billionth of a moment. Then...

POP!

The lid shot up into the air like a cork out of a volcano.

WHOOOOOOSHHHHH!

A living mass of moldy rags and putrid potato peels rose up and out of the can, swinging its arms like a blind zombie.

FLASH!

The night lit up with the glare of four floodlights.

CLICK! CLICK! CLICK!

With light flooding the garbage cans, Vicki snapped photo after photo. These were going to be the most amazing pictures of her life!

At first, the Abominable Trashman was stunned by the sudden blast of light. Then he became angry, leaped out of the garbage can, and headed straight for Vicki.

Vicki stumbled backward, tripped over a stone, and landed on her back. But she scrambled right back up and made a run for it. She could smell the breath of the monster as he closed in on her. It smelled like spoiled cabbage, year-old stew, and a plate of moldy anchovies.

Just when Vicki thought she was going to get away, something snagged the strap on her camera. She was yanked backward, like a fish on a hook.

"HELLLLLPPPP!" The Abominable Trashman had her in his gloppy clutches.

"Larry! *Help me!*"

Vicki cast a terrified look over her shoulder, expecting to see Larry running to her aid. Instead, he was running in the opposite direction. Larry the Janitor vanished into the trees, leaving Vicki all alone to face the monster.

CHAPTER 5

MONSTER MASH

Vicki's life flashed before her eyes like a movie with coming attractions of heaven. The Abominable Trashman smashed her camera to bits and dragged her back toward the garbage can. But just at that moment, something zipped from out of the darkness.

THONK!

A plunger came flying from the trees and caught the monster square in the back.

"Prepare to be recycled, banana breath!" Those brave words came from none other than the Veggie defender—Larryboy! The caped cucumber hopped out of the bushes and struck a heroic pose.

Unfortunately, he spent a little too long posing. The monster ripped the plunger from his back and hurled it back at Larryboy like a harpoon. Catching Larryboy right in the kisser, it completely covered his face. What's worse, Larryboy couldn't pull the supersuction plunger off, causing an instant blackout—Larryboy couldn't see anything.

The monster heaved Vicki aside and closed in on our purple hero. Larryboy could smell him coming.

With a daring back flip, Larryboy avoided the monster and fired off his second plunger ear. The heat-seeking plunger zeroed in on the monster with incredible accuracy.

THONK!

The plunger hit the Abominable Trashman squarely in the mug, completely covering his face.

This put the two opponents in an interesting spot. Larryboy still couldn't see. But now the Abominable Trashman couldn't see either. Stranger yet, Larryboy and the Trashman were connected to each other by the cords attached to each plunger.

"Time to take out the trash, man!" Larryboy shouted as he blindly ran into a tree.

"ROARRRR!" the Trashman bellowed as he blindly banged into the side of the garage.

"Prepare to be trashed, anchovy arms!" Larryboy

yelled, giving a karate kick to the tree. He followed up with two head butts. "That's a tree!" Vicki shouted. "It's not the Trashman!"

"Boy, am I glad to hear that," Larryboy said, shaking his noggin. "I thought this guy had abs of steel!" Then our purple-headed hero did a triple spin in the air and declared, "Prepare to do the dance of doom, Monster Mash!"

Only one problem. After all of this spinning, Larryboy and the Abominable Trashman got all tangled up in Larryboy's plunger cords. The two were tied up, back-to-back.

"Vicki, where is he now?" Larryboy shouted.

"He's right behind you!"

Still blinded by the plunger, Larryboy spun around to face the monster. But because the Trashman was strapped to Larryboy's back, when our hero spun around, so did the Abominable Trashman.

"Take that, you rotten rascal!" said Larryboy as he lunged forward again, but caught nothing but air.

"Where'd he go, Vicki? Where'd he go?"

"He's right behind you, Larryboy!"

"Boy, this monster is quick!"

Larryboy spun around again.

"Now where is he, Vicki?"

"Behind you!"

"And now?"

"He's still behind you!"

This happened about ten times before Larryboy realized that this strategy might not work.

The monster's smell was stronger than ten skunks with hygiene problems, but Larryboy was prepared. He was wearing his "Ocean-Mist Utility Belt." One push of the button and out popped a can of deodorant, a bar of scented soap, a container of potpourri (ask your mom what that is), and two cans of ... *laser-guided air freshener!*

Larryboy fired double-barreled squirts of air freshener, and the air around the monster melted into scents of lilacs and roses.

It drove the Abominable Trashman absolutely nutty.

Swatting at the cloud of flowery air freshener, the monster roared, coughed, and tore at the cords that bound him. When the cords were finally shredded, the Trashman leaped back inside the garbage can and disappeared into the night.

Everything was quiet once again. Vicki was so happy to be alive that she didn't even care that her camera had been destroyed, along with the photos in it.

"Larryboy! That was the bravest thing I've ever seen anyone do!" she said, her eyes glittering in the floodlight. "That took more courage than Phil Winklesteen jumping into Bumbly Bay to save those seven puppies!"

Larryboy blushed beneath his mask. "Aw, gee Vicki, it was nothing."

"It was much more than nothing! It was Larry the Janitor who did nothing! I'm very disappointed in him. He left me all alone with that monster!"

Vicki's words stung. "But Vicki, don't be so hard on Larry. He did—"

"What? He didn't do *anything* to help me. But *you*—you were incredibly brave!"

Larryboy was speechless. He didn't know what to say. Larryboy was a success. But Larry the Janitor was a failure in Vicki's eyes.

CHAPTER 6

SLAVES TO FEAR

Leaving Larryboy to ponder his predicament, we now go deep below the streets of Bumblyburg.

All kinds of supervillains had built their secret lairs beneath the city, including the onion-headed master criminal of all time, Awful Alvin. Alvin's lair had it all—built-in shark pools, piranha tanks, and a dining-room table with a trapdoor beneath every chair. In fact, Alvin's lair was so amazing that it had even appeared on the cover of the magazine *Better Lairs and Gardens*.

Awful Alvin was in an awfully good mood. He was singing karaoke to the song "B-Burg, B-Burg, What an Abominable Town." He was also dancing around the lair with his partner in crime, Lampy—a sidekick who happened to be...well...a lamp.

"My plan is working flawlessly," Alvin cackled as he tap-danced on top of his coffee table. "I have created the perfect monster, and now everyone in Bumblyburg is too scared to take out the trash! What do you think of that, Lampy?"

Lampy didn't answer. Lamps don't usually have much to say.

"Dance with me, Lampy!" Alvin shouted as he twirled Lampy into the next room, where a television studio had been set up. Hundreds of TV sets filled one huge wall, each of them showing pictures of different garbage cans in town.

"I've struck fear in the lives of the citizens of Bumblyburg! When I make people afraid, I have them in my power!" Alvin explained as he wheeled a television camera into the room for Lampy to see. "And when I have people in my power, they'll do *anything* I tell them to do! They're slaves to their fear! And that makes them slaves to *me!* HA-HA-HA-HA-HA-HA!"

Alvin set Lampy in front of the television camera and dabbed some makeup on the lampshade.

"Today, you're going to be a TV star, Lampy!" Alvin shouted with diabolical glee. "I'd like you to announce my evil plan to all of Bumblyburg—on prime-time TV. I've even made some cue cards for you!"

Alvin held up the cards, upon which he had scribbled, in crayon, the words that Lampy was to read. Then Awful Alvin turned on the television camera, counted down from five, and pointed at Lampy.

"You're on, Lampy! Lights! Camera! Villainy!"

CHAPTER 7

AND NOW A WORD FROM OUR BLACKMAILERS...

Meanwhile, Larryboy sipped iced tea as he watched his favorite television show.

"That Jethro just cracks me up," Larryboy said to his butler, Archie, who also happened to be an amazing inventor and high-tech wiz.

"I'm pleased to hear that, Master Larry," said Archie, who sat nearby. "However, I couldn't help but notice that you're not laughing out loud and iced tea isn't shooting out of your nose, like it normally does when you watch that show."

There was a long pause.

"You're right, Archie," Larryboy said, spinning around to face his friend. "I admit it. I'm still bothered by what Vicki said to me last night.

She said she was very disappointed in Larry the Janitor! She thinks I'm afraid!"

"Well, you did say she saw you run into the bushes," Archie observed.

"Then maybe I should tell her that Larry the Janitor and Larryboy are the same person. I'm afraid that if I don't, she'll never talk to Larry the Janitor again!"

Archie quickly turned to face Larryboy. "Tell her your secret identity? I would not advise that, Master Larry."

"But I'm afraid that—"

"You're just going to have to deal with it. You're going to have to—"

Suddenly, Larryboy's show vanished from the TV. In its place, the silent image of a lamp popped onto the screen. But it wasn't just any old lamp.

"Hey look, Archie!" said Larryboy. "It's Lampy! What's he doing on TV?"

"That's most unusual," Archie agreed, pulling up his seat next to Larryboy. "Lampy is usually rather shy."

Larryboy and Archie sat in the darkened cave, watching the image of Lampy. But there was no sound.

"Nothing's happening," Larryboy whispered to Archie.

"Why isn't there any sound?"

At that instant, Awful Alvin appeared on the screen and shouted, "Turn on the closed captioning! The closed captioning!"

"Oh. Right. Closed captioning," Larryboy said, pointing his remote at the television. By pushing the closed-captioning button, the following words could be seen, being scrolled along the bottom of the screen:

People of Bumblyburg, be afraid. Be very afraid. Awful Alvin has created the most fearsome creature to ever appear in a garbage can (even scarier than used tissue)! I speak, of course, of the Abominable Trashman.

The Abominable Trashman will continue to terrify your city unless you become his slaves. And as his slaves, you must do certain things for him...or else!

1. Get rid of all real, rubber, or plush chickens (any pictures of them too).

2. Throw away all polyester pants.

3. Every night, stand outside the house,

wearing a lampshade on your head while

holding a bright light. Anyone who does not

obey these rules will receive a visit from the

Abominable Trashman! Be afraid. Be very

afraid! **HA-HA-HA-HA!**

We now return you to your regularly

scheduled program.

Lampy vanished from the screen in a storm of static.

"I don't like the looks of this," said Larryboy. "I really

enjoy my polyester leisure suit."

"Those are certainly strange demands," said Archie. "But look here, Master Larry. I think I may have discovered something."

Larryboy looked over Archie's shoulder at the computer screen. "What are those squiggly red lines crisscrossing your map of Bumblyburg?"

"They're underground tunnels," Archie explained. "And the tunnels run to every house in Bumblyburg. If my calculations are correct, I believe the tunnels are connected to the new garbage cans that have been sprouting up all around town."

"You mean…?"

"Yes! That's how the monster is appearing in garbage cans everywhere. The monster crawls through the tunnels and jumps out of the cans!"

"You mean…?"

"Yes! The only way we'll be able to stop the monster is if you drop into one of the trash cans, crawl through the tunnels, and track down the creature!"

"You mean…?"

"Yes! That means you're going to have to conquer your fear of small, enclosed spaces."

Larryboy gulped. He hated tight spaces. In fact, that's one of the main reasons why Larryboy was terrified of using the secret pneumatic Larrytube transporter—a tube that could carry him from the newspaper office to the Larrycave in the blink of an eye.

Larryboy was afraid. He was very afraid.

CHAPTER 8

A SECRET-IDENTITY CRISIS

The next morning, when Larry the Janitor arrived at the *Daily Bumble*, he saw Vicki working at her desk. This was his chance to make things right with her. But Vicki left right away, as if she were trying to avoid him.

Larry didn't track her down until the end of the day, when he found her at the water cooler.

"Vicki, you don't understand what happened the other night," Larry said, desperately.

"I understand perfectly. You got frightened and left me in the clutches of a monster. What else is there to say?"

"But there's another side of me that's very brave," Larry insisted. "You just don't know it."

Vicki shook her head sadly and sighed.

Then, as she hopped away, she said over her shoulder, "I've got photos to take, Larry. Maybe we can talk later."

There had to be something that Larry could do to prove to Vicki that he wasn't a complete chicken. If only he could tell her that he was Larryboy. If only he could tell her that the reason he ran away was to change into his superhero costume!

It was so tempting….Maybe he could tell her…. maybe…just maybe…

He decided to do it.

Before he could change his mind, Larry yanked a piece of paper from Bob's desk and scribbled it all down. In the note, he told Vicki that *he* was Larryboy. *He* was that hero of Bumblyburg! *He* was the one who battled the Abominable Trashman.

Trying not to think about what he was doing, Larry sealed the envelope, stuck the letter on Vicki's desk, and then dashed outside.

Larry felt good about what he had done…for about two minutes. But with every step he took closer to home, a different question popped into his mind.

What if Vicki tells her friends? What if Vicki reveals my

secret in a news story? And what will happen if every vil-lain learns my secret identity?

Suddenly, Larry came to a dead stop. His eyes bugged out. "*What have I done?*"

Wheeling around, Larry tore back to the newspaper. He had to get that letter back! He just had to!

He sprinted up five flights of stairs, burst into the newsroom, knocked over Bob the Tomato, and sent papers flying everywhere. He scrambled to Vicki's cubicle and dove toward her desk. Where was it? *Where was it?*

The letter was gone...and so was Vicki.

His secret was out.

CHAPTER 9

THE SUBSTITUTE MONSTER

That night, Larryboy crept into his weekly Superhero 101 class at Bumblyburg Community College—the only class in the world for vegetables with powers far beyond those of normal Veggies. He was afraid that his classmates would somehow learn that he had broken one of the biggest superhero rules: never give away your secret identity.

So, with worries eating away at him, today's lesson was quite fitting: "How Superheroes Battle Fear."

Unfortunately, the class professor, the wise and wonderful Bok Choy, was gone that evening.

When the superheroes arrived, they found a message scrawled on the blackboard: "Bok Choy cannot make it tonight. Your substitute teacher will be Miss Eville." (It also looked like someone had written and then erased **"HA-HA-HA-HA!"**.)

"I don't like the looks of this," Larryboy whispered to Lemon Twist, the superhero girl in the seat next to him. "Where's our substitute?"

There was absolutely no sign of the substitute teacher—just an empty chair at the front of the room.

"I was a substitute teacher once," said the Scarlet Tomato, "at a junior high. Talk about scary. I would never have survived all those spitballs without my superpowers."

"I've never heard of Miss Eville," griped Electro-Melon, a hulking fruit with anger-management problems.

Five minutes passed. Still no sign of the teacher.

"I say we call it a night," suggested Larryboy, gathering up his Superhero Handbook.

But before he could rise from his seat, the classroom door slammed shut and locked—all by itself. Then the windows came sliding down and the lights went out, plunging the room into darkness. There was no escape.

A lot of superhero hearts suddenly began to beat superfast.

"I knew I should have taken Superhero Cape

Crocheting 101 this semester," said Larryboy.

Panic was rising fast. And then the garbage can near the front of the room began to shake, rattle, and roll.

"It's the Abominable Trashman!"

The fear was so thick that you could cut it with a knife. You could even scoop it with a spoon, flip it with a spatula, or pick it up with chopsticks.

"Hold it, you guys!" Larryboy shouted. "We're superheroes! We can't be pushed around by one little garbage monster!"

"Good point."

"Hadn't thought about that."

So the superheroes did what every superhero does in a sticky situation. They used their superpowers. Electro-Melon fired up his electrical field. Lemon Twist unleashed her tornado powers. And Larryboy launched his plunger ears.

"OK class, that's enough. Settle down now," came a calm voice by the door. The lights flicked back on, and there stood Bok Choy.

"Bok Choy! We thought you couldn't make it."

"So sorry," said Bok Choy. "There was never really going to be a substitute teacher. Instead, I was giving you a pop quiz. But first let me thank the Invisible Carrot Twins for their help."

Two invisible carrot superheroes slowly materialized in front of the classroom and bowed. They were the ones who had closed the door and windows and made the garbage can rattle.

"How many of you felt fear just now?" asked Bok Choy.

At first, no one answered.

"It's OK to admit it."

"Well...I guess I did say that I wished I had taken Superhero Cape Crocheting," Larryboy admitted, a little embarrassed.

"It's OK to feel fear," Bok Choy said. "Being brave doesn't mean that you never feel fearful. When you're faced by a villain with the power to squash you flat, who wouldn't be afraid?" Bok Choy went on to explain that what makes people brave is how they respond to fear. Do they let fear control them? Do they make wrong decisions when they're afraid? Or do they continue to do the right thing, even when they're scared?

Bok Choy asked the class to open their Superhero Handbooks to Section 19, Paragraph 34, Line 4. The handbook said: "I looked to the LORD, and he answered me. He saved me from everything I was afraid of."

"God will give you brave hearts, even when you're scared silly," said Bok Choy, walking over to the windows. "Look! The people of Bumblyburg have been scared into extreme silliness."

Through the windows, the entire class could see Bumblyburg citizens dumping garbage into their yards because they were too afraid to take it to their trash cans. They could also see people standing outside of their houses with lampshades on their heads while holding bright lights—just as Awful Alvin had ordered.

Like obedient slaves, people did everything Alvin told them to do. They frantically tore pictures of chickens out of their cookbooks and threw them out with the garbage, along with every piece of polyester clothing. Anyone who didn't obey was paid a visit by the Abominable Trashman.

"Fear is taking over the city," said Bok Choy. "It must be stopped."

CHAPTER 10

ROCKET-BOY

"Are you sure this thing is going to work?" Larryboy asked Archie the next day.

"Well...I haven't ironed out all of the kinks in the Larrysled," said Archie. "But we have no choice but to act now."

"Kinks? I don't like the sound of kinks."

The Larrysled was a slick, purple sled with super-suction wheels—perfect for rolling through tunnels at incredibly high speeds. A large rocket was attached to each side.

"If Bob were doing this, we'd call it a Bobsled," Archie joked. But Larryboy was too nervous to laugh.

Archie had also created what looked like an astronaut's space helmet for Larryboy. A little, green, tree-shaped air freshener dangled inside the plastic helmet (important for anyone submerged in week-old glop).

Larryboy waddled over to the garbage can behind the Larrycave—a portal into Awful Alvin's network of tunnels. Then he pushed the orange button on his sled, and the two rockets fired up.

"Well...I guess this is it, Archie old friend," he said, staring into the open garbage can. Larryboy felt like he was about to dive into the intestines of a giant worm. "Tight spaces," he said, woozy with fear. "Why do these tunnels have to be such tight spaces?"

"Remember, Larryboy, God will give you a brave heart to do what's right, even when you're scared silly."

With the flaming Larrysled in his clutches, Larryboy and the rocket-sled teetered on the edge of the garbage can— like someone too afraid to jump off of the diving board. "Are you sure that Lemon Twist isn't interested in this job?"

"You can do it, Master Larry," said Archie, running down the to-do list on his clipboard. Unfortunately, as Archie looked down at his clipboard, he wasn't watching where he was going. He bumped smack into the back of the Larrysled.

BOINKK!

"AHHHHHHHHHHHHHHHHH!"

That was Larryboy screaming, in case you hadn't
already guessed.

The caped cucumber was knocked forward, fell belly-
down on his Larrysled, and tumbled into the bottomless can
of disgusting yuk, moldering muck, and decaying gluck.

"Oops," said Archie, staring into the hole at the bottom
of the garbage can. "My bad."

Riding the Larrysled, Larryboy roared through a tunnel
of rubbish and rot. With blinding speed, he tore through
piles of broken toys, decaying food, plastic wrappers, and
half-eaten candy bars.

"Are you all right, Larryboy?" came Archie's voice over
a radio built into the helmet.

"I'm OK, Archie. But things are pretty gross down here!"

Larryboy zipped like a purple bullet through the tunnels beneath Bumblyburg. Around and around and around
and around he raced, as if he were on a never-ending
roller-coaster ride. Some of the tunnels were packed with
garbage, which smacked against Larryboy's plastic helmet
like bugs on a windshield. But other tunnels were clear

sailing and completely free of trash.

"Archie! How do I steer this thing?"

"Use the joystick!" Archie yelled.

"But I'm feeling no joy!" Larryboy yelled, pushing the stick to the right. The Larrysled made a screaming right turn down a new tunnel.

"New problem, Archie."

"What's that, Master Larry?"

"This tunnel has a dead end—emphasis on the word *dead*. How do I stop this thing?"

There was silence for what seemed like forever. "OK, now I remember what that kink in the sled is."

"You mean I can't stop?"

"No, but you can eject. Push the yellow button."

Larryboy pushed the yellow button and out popped a

steaming cup of hot cocoa, served by a robotic arm.

"Sorry," Archie said. "I had that installed for the Larrysled that used to be a snow sled. It was really nice on cold days."

"*Archie!*"

Not far ahead was a solid wall of dirt where the tunnel ended.

"Try the mauve-colored button."

"What color is mauve?" Larryboy asked, frantically pushing every button in sight. The red button controlled the CD player. The blue button served snow cones. The wall was only seconds away.

Larryboy was about to find out what it's like to be a crash-test dummy.

Finally, he jammed down the mauve-colored button, but by then it was too late. The Larrysled hit the wall with such speed that not even a cartoon character could have survived such a crash.

Not even Larryboy.

CHAPTER 11

HEAPS OF TROUBLE

It was a good thing the dirt wall was just a hologram—a 3-D illusion. It wasn't really there.

Larryboy ejected from the Larrysled as it soared through the hologram wall and entered an underground room of some sort. The caped cucumber landed in a huge heap of garbage, while the rocket-sled bored through another mound of trash, hit a real wall...and exploded.

"*Larryboy! Are you OK?*" shouted a frantic Archie over the radio.

"Just fine, Archie. But I'm afraid your Larrysled has seen its last slope. Where am I?"

Larryboy glanced around, knowing that Archie could see through the camera mounted on his helmet.

It was an enormous,

brightly lit room, filled with many mounds of moldering garbage. Millions of flies danced around the trash. (They were doing the jitterbug.) It was a good thing that Larry-boy's helmet hadn't cracked, because the smell in the room was enough to stun a full-grown yak with sinus problems.

"My computer shows that the room is connected to Awful Alvin's lair," said Archie. "This must be where Alvin stores the garbage that he stuffs into his tunnels."

"Why does he even bother stuffing his tunnels with trash?"

"To keep people out. You'd have to be incredibly foolish to enter tunnels packed with foul garbage."

"Gee thanks, Archie."

"You know what I mean."

Larryboy scanned the huge room. "I don't see the Abominable Trashman down here," said Larryboy. "So what do I do now?"

Before Archie could answer, all of the lights in the room suddenly went off, plunging Larryboy into darkness.

"What happened, Larryboy? Have I lost the video feed?"

"No. But I've lost all light. I don't like this, Archie. It's downright creepy."

"Use the flashlight mounted on top of your helmet. And remember what Bok Choy told you. It's OK to be afraid. Just don't be a slave to your fear. Keep your head."

"I plan to. It's the only one I've got."

Larryboy clicked on the flashlight and continued to explore with his meager beam of brightness. In the dark, every sound became sharper.

The dripping of water.

The buzz of flies.

The soft steps of someone approaching.

Someone approaching?

Larryboy's heart leaped, and then the alarm built into Larryboy's helmet suddenly started blaring—like a car alarm, but even more annoying.

Trouble was coming.

CHAPTER 12

THERE'S NOTHING TO FEAR BUT FEAR ITSELF (BUT I CAN THINK OF A FEW OTHER THINGS)

Trouble arrived.

Larryboy spun around with cat-like reflexes, fired both of his plungers, knocked the trash monster on his back, tied him up with a sturdy rope, and dragged him to Officer Olaf's paddy wagon.

Well...not quite. That was the way Larryboy imagined it would go.

The real event was a bit tougher.

In truth, the Abominable Trashman pounced on Larryboy from behind, wrapping his slimy arms around him. Larryboy tried to fire both of his plungers. But there was one slight problem. You can't fire supersuction ears when your head is completely covered by a clear, plastic helmet. The suction cups hit the sides of the plastic helmet and attached themselves.

"Sorry, Larryboy," said Archie over the radio. "Finding a way for you to fire your supersuction ears while wearing the helmet was on my to-do list."

"OUCH."

Then the Trashman yanked Larryboy's helmet off, destroying his radio connection to Archie and causing his supersuction ears to retract with a **THOP!** Then he dragged our hero down a long hallway, swung open a heavy, steel door, and hurled Larryboy into a cold and moldy prison cell. The door slammed shut with a **CLANG** that echoed down the hallway.

"Boy, are you a sight for sore eyes," came a voice that startled Larryboy. He wasn't expecting a familiar voice this deep underground.

Larryboy looked up from the floor and blinked twice to make sure he wasn't seeing things.

"Hello, Larryboy," said Vicki Cucumber.

CHAPTER 13

A TRASH-COMPACTION, ACTION HERO

"Vicki! What are you doing here?"

"Just trying to take some photographs," Vicki said. "After my last camera was destroyed, I tried to get new photos of the Abominable Trashman. But that guy really doesn't like having his picture taken."

"I guess I wouldn't want my picture taken if I had stale pizza crusts for a face," said Larryboy, trying to stop his eyeballs from rolling around in their sockets.

"Anyway, the creature caught me and dragged me down here. And I've lost another company camera. Bob's not going to be happy."

Vicki nodded toward the corner, where her smashed camera lay in a big pile of trash.

But what caught Larryboy's eye

was Vicki's camera bag. A letter stuck out of the side pocket. It was Larry's letter! The letter in which he revealed his secret identity!

Larryboy couldn't tell if the letter had been opened or not.

"So how's the weather?" Larryboy said, trying to make small talk as he sidled over toward the camera bag to get a closer look.

"Say cheese, Larryboy!"

A flash went off, catching Larryboy just as he was bending down for a closer look at the envelope. Startled, Larryboy bolted back upright.

"What was *that?*"

"My other camera. Fortunately, I had a spare, mini-camera hidden in my pocket," said Vicki, beaming.

Larryboy smiled weakly. Suddenly, loud voices could be heard from just outside the prison cell. It sounded like people were arguing.

"This could be important," Larryboy said. "Good thing Archie built a listening device into my supersuction ears."

Larryboy fired one of his ears against the cell wall with a **THONK** and began to listen.

"I can't do it," he heard someone saying. It sounded like the Trashman.

"You have no choice. You're my slave!" said another voice. This one Larryboy recognized.

"It's Awful Alvin," Larryboy whispered to Vicki. "Quick, listen in on my other ear."

Vicki pulled out Larryboy's other supersuction ear and listened through it like it was an old-fashioned telephone.

"But I don't want to hurt the poor cucumber lady or the purple plunger boy," said the Abominable Trashman.

"Why? Larryboy attacked you with air freshener, which you're awfully allergic to!" Alvin said.

"He was just protecting the cucumber lady."

"Do you want me to tell the world your secret?" snarled Awful Alvin.

"*No!* Anything but that!"

"I thought as much," Alvin cackled. (Every villain has to get in his minimum daily allowance of cackling.) "Your fans wouldn't be too happy if they heard that those seven puppies saved *you* from Bumbly Bay—not the other way around!"

"Please don't tell anybody! Please!" begged the

Abominable Trashman.

"I can see the headline now: 'Phil Winklesteen Saved by Puppies!' Your movie career would be over."

"That's what I'm afraid of," whimpered the Trashman.

Could it be true? Was the Abominable Trashman really Phil Winklesteen, the famous action-movie hero from Toledo, Ohio?

"This is amazing," Vicki whispered to Larryboy. "Winklesteen is a celery. So if he's the Trashman, he must be wearing a monster suit of some sort. And his monster arms must be mechanical."

"Ssshhh, they're talking again," said Larryboy.

"Admit it, Winklesteen. You're a slave to your fear," snarled Awful Alvin. "So obey me, and do your job."

"Yes, Master."

Larryboy and Vicki heard what sounded like a heavy lever being yanked. But here's the awful part. The walls of the prison cell began to shake. The gears of a machine groaned from under the floor. And then the walls of the room began to move.

They began to move *inward*.

"Now I know what this room reminds me of," said Vicki.

"It's a giant trash compactor!"

They were about to be smashed like peanut butter and jelly between two giant slabs of concrete bread.

CHAPTER 14

PANIC ROOM

"HA-HA-HA-HA-HA!" cackled Awful Alvin. "When you're gone, Larryboy, no one will be able to stop me from turning every person in this city into my slave!"

Larryboy stuck his face up to a tiny opening in the door to the room—an opening as narrow as a mail slot. "Lampy, you can't let Alvin do this to us!" he shouted to Alvin's sidekick.

"Don't listen to him, Lampy," said Alvin. "It's time we put an end to this purple-headed pest. Come on, Lampy! Let's get out of here!"

"Uh...Larryboy...," said Vicki.

"Lampy, if you turn off this giant trash compactor, I'll buy you a twenty-foot extension cord."

"Uh...Larryboy... "

"Come on, Lampy! Don't let Alvin—"

"*Larryboy!*" Vicki shouted.

"What is it?" Larryboy asked, turning away from the opening in the door.

"You're talking to a lamp."

Larryboy stopped to think for a moment. "Oh. Right. I suppose that's not the wisest use of my time."

"That's what I was thinking, Larry," Vicki said.

"*Larry?* Did you just call me *Larry?*"

Vicki looked shocked. "I mean Larryboy! We've got to find a way out of here, Larryboy!"

Larryboy paused. She knew!

But Larryboy couldn't think about that now. Alvin and Lampy had disappeared down a hallway, leaving Phil Winklesteen (the Trashman) to stand guard.

The caped cucumber struck a dramatic pose. "Have no fear, Vicki, my dear."

Larryboy dug through the mound of trash in the room, pulled a bamboo fishing pole out of the pile, and propped it between the two moving walls.

SNAP!

The fishing pole broke like a giant toothpick.

The walls were now only about ten feet apart and closing in.

"You've got to help us, Mr. Winklesteen!" Vicki yelled through the tiny slit in the door. "You can't just let us be squashed flat like pancakes!"

Vicki could hear Phil Winklesteen moving around just outside the door, but he didn't answer.

"OK, so maybe you didn't save those puppies from Bumbly Bay," shouted Vicki. "But don't be a slave to your fear! God will give you a brave heart to do what's right, even when you're scared silly! This is your chance to show some real courage!"

No answer.

The concrete walls were now about eight feet apart. The gears underneath the floor groaned like mechanical monsters.

Larryboy pulled a discarded surfboard out of the trash and propped it between the walls.

CRACK!

The surfboard snapped into five pieces.

"Phil, if you're afraid to rescue us, that's OK!" Larryboy shouted. "Even superheroes like me are afraid sometimes— actually, right now comes to mind. But God can help us to be brave, even when we're scared silly!"

No answer.

The concrete walls were now about six feet apart, inching forward like deadly, concrete glaciers.

Larryboy tried to jam an inflatable rubber raft between the walls.

POP!

"Where's a steel pole when you need one?" Larryboy griped, digging through the trash.

"You've got to help us, Phil!" Vicki yelled.

In desperation, Larryboy shouted the words that he remembered from Bok Choy: "I looked to the Lord, and he answered me! He saved me from everything I was afraid of!"

Inspired by those words, Larryboy did the only thing left to do. He propped himself between the two walls. With the bottom of his cucumber body against one wall and his purple, plunger-eared head against the other wall, our hero gritted his teeth. Vicki marveled at his courage.

She also took a few snapshots.

"Can you make double prints for me?" Larryboy asked. "I'd love a copy for my wallet."

The squeeze was on.

CHAPTER 15

UNMASKING A MONSTER

"I'm doing it!" Larryboy declared in triumph. "It's actually working!"

With Larryboy's body propped in between them, the walls had suddenly stopped moving inward. Amazing!

"Uh...Larryboy..." said Vicki.

"This is incredible!"

"Uh...Larryboy..."

"I have greater powers than I imagined!"

"Uh...Larryboy...Look over here," said Vicki.

Larryboy glanced sideways. The door to the trash-compactor room was wide open. Standing in the doorway was Phil Winklesteen, with his Trashman mask removed.

"Phil turned off the trash compactor," Vicki pointed out. "He's rescuing us."

Larryboy smiled. "I knew that."

"Is it too late to be courageous?" Phil asked.

"It's never too late!" Larryboy shouted, dropping to the ground and striking a dramatic pose.

"Then let's get going!" Phil beamed.

They dashed out of the room and hurried through a secret exit.

"This is great!" Larryboy said. "Once people see that the Abominable Trashman is really Phil Winklesteen, a celery from Toledo, they won't be slaves to their fears anymore. Awful Alvin will no longer control them."

It all seemed too easy.

The three heroes clambered up a metal ladder. Then Phil shoved open a hatch in the roof, which led back above ground. Larryboy bounded through the hatch and struck a dramatic pose, his cape flapping in the breeze.

One second later, his heart sank, and his cape stopped flapping. What Larryboy saw terrified him to the core.

Standing tall over Bumblyburg was another trash monster. Only this monster was a zillion times larger than Phil Winklesteen. This creature was as tall as a five-story building.

It was tall enough to destroy an entire city.

CHAPTER 16

GUNKZILLA

The new monster was a super-sized version of the Abominable Trashman—but much bigger and much more dangerous. *Gunkzilla* was a more fitting name for this monstrous creature.

As Gunkzilla stomped through downtown Bumblyburg, walls crumbled. The earth shook. Veggies fled in all directions. Fear had completely taken over the city.

Correction. Awful Alvin had completely taken over Bumblyburg.

"Winklesteen, did you think you were going to be my one and only monster?" came an evil voice from right behind our heroes. Larryboy, Vicki, and Phil spun around to see Awful Alvin (and Lampy) just yards away in their hovercraft.

"How...how did you do this?" Phil asked.

"I'm glad you asked," Alvin said, eager to brag. "You see, I used you, Phil. I used you to strike fear in the citizens of Bumblyburg. And then I used that fear to power my greatest invention ever—the Trash Reenergizer."

"And what in the world is that?" scowled Vicki.

"The Trash Reenergizer can make garbage come alive and take any shape I want," Alvin cackled. "And it's powered by fear. My machine sucks up people's fear and uses that power to create monsters out of trash. The result is even more fear. You might say it recycles fear. It's very energy efficient."

"A machine that makes trash monsters? This I have to see," said Larryboy. "Where do you keep it?"

"Do you think I'd be ridiculous enough to tell you where

I keep my secret weapon?"

"Why, yes," said Larryboy. "You just told us your entire evil plot."

"Explaining evil plots is required of all villains near the end of stories," Alvin explained. "But the Association of Supervillains does not require us to tell the location of our secret weapons. That's for you to find out." Awful Alvin cackled for what had to have been the fiftieth time that day. (He was close to setting the world record for cackling.) *Be afraid, Larryboy! Be very afraid!"* Awful Alvin shouted. Then he and Lampy took off in their hovercraft and blazed across the afternoon sky.

"This is all my fault," Phil groaned. "I stirred up fear in Bumblyburg. Now that fear is being used to power Alvin's awful machine. And that machine is being used to create giant trash monsters."

"I just wish we knew what Awful Alvin was afraid of," said Larryboy. "That would come in handy."

Phil blinked in surprise. "You mean you don't know?"

"Well ... no. Do you?"

"I thought everybody knew," Phil said. "Awful Alvin has 'alektorophobia,' which is the fear of chickens, and 'noctiphobia,' the fear of darkness. He even has 'textophobia,' which is the fear of fabrics—in his case, polyester."

"So that's why he's been forcing people to rid the city of chickens and polyester pants!" Vicki exclaimed. "And that's why he's been forcing people to wear lampshades and stand around at night with bright lights!"

"Absolutely. He's trying to rid Bumblyburg of everything *he's* afraid of."

"This changes everything," Larryboy said, a gleam coming to his eyes. "Here's what I want you guys to do." Quickly, Larryboy told Phil and Vicki his cunning idea and then added, "I've got to find Archie. It's time to take out some trash!"

CHAPTER 17

BRAVE HEARTS

When Larryboy reached the Larrycave, he found

that Archie already had the Larryplane ready to fly.

Larryboy leaped into the cockpit and raced toward the

heart of Bumblyburg.

Finding his first target was easy. He simply had to

look for a living pile of garbage five stories high.

Gunkzilla had just stepped on a parked car and was try-

ing to shake it loose from the bottom of his foot.

The Larryplane swooped right by the head of the

trashy monster, like a pesky fly. The creature tried

to swat the plane, but he wasn't quick enough.

Larryboy brought the plane around for a sec-

ond pass and fired four

plungers, two from each wing.

The four plungers were magnetized, so they zipped straight for the metal belly of Gunkzilla.

THONK! THONK! THONK! THONK!

"ROWRRRR!" (That's monster for "Oooo, that tickles!")

With the plungers connected to the belly of the beast, Larryboy circled Gunkzilla. Once. Twice. Three times. Every time he circled the monster, the tether lines attached to the plungers wrapped around the large arms of Gunkzilla, tying him up like a bundle of...well...trash.

The monster couldn't budge.

"That'll hold him for a little while. Now it's time to pay a visit to Awful Alvin," Larryboy told Archie over his radio.

"My radar has tracked Alvin's movements," Archie said over the communicator. "He's hiding in the Bumbly Mountains, fourth cave from the left."

Larryboy knew the exact cave. The Not Welcome mat in front of the cave was a dead giveaway.

"So *this* is the Trash Reenergizer," said Larryboy, stepping into the brightly lit cave where Alvin was hiding. In one corner was a huge machine, which looked like it had been built out of junk from the local garbage dump. On top of the contraption was a giant satellite dish, which

soaked up fear and powered the machine. (It also brought in five hundred television stations, including the All-Fish-Slapping Network.)

Awful Alvin whirled around. "Rats! What are you doing here, Larryboy?"

"I'm shutting you down, Awful Alvin."

"That's what you think." An evil gleam glittered in his oniony eyes. Alvin turned to his trusty sidekick and said,

"There's one thing this superhero didn't plan on, isn't there, Lampy?"

"And what's that?" asked Larryboy.

"*This!*"

Awful Alvin pulled a huge switch on the wall. A garbage can, hanging upside down above Larryboy's head, suddenly dropped from the ceiling before our hero could even react. The can slammed down over Larryboy, trapping him inside.

"You've seen how my Trash Reenergizer can turn ordinary garbage into living monsters," Awful Alvin said with a twisted grin. "What you didn't know is that I can reverse the process. I can also turn living things...into trash!"

With a diabolical laugh, Alvin yanked another humongous lever. Sparks showered down from the ceiling. Bolts of electricity danced alongside the garbage can. Smoke filled the cave.

Then Awful Alvin slowly raised the garbage can.

Larryboy was gone. In his place was a tiny mound of bubblegum wrappers, apple cores, and burned popcorn. Trash. That was all that was left of Larryboy.

CHAPTER 18

CHICKEN!

"AHHHHHHHHHHH!"

Vicki screamed.

She and Phil Winklesteen ran into the cave at the exact moment that Awful Alvin changed Larryboy into a pile of trash. Vicki couldn't believe her eyes.

"AHHHHHHHHHHHHH!" That was Awful Alvin's scream. (If you put your ear close to the page, you can tell the difference.)

Why was Alvin screaming? Well, because Phil and Vicki had collected a dozen chickens. And those chickens were standing in the mouth of the cave like gunslingers at a showdown in an old-time Western.

"BWAKKK! BWAKKK! BWAKKK!" (Those were the chickens clucking, in case you hadn't already guessed.)

Awful Alvin had been terrified of chick-

ens ever since he was five years old, when a chicken mistook his oniony head for an egg. The chicken sat on his head for two days, and he hasn't been the same since.

"AHHHHHHHHHH!" Awful Alvin screamed a second time.

"AHHHHHHHHHH!" So did Vicki.

Then total chaos ensued. Awful Alvin picked up Lampy and sprinted out of the cave, screaming like a maniac. The chickens, sensing his fear, went after him like something out of the classic movie, *Attack from Planet Chicken!*

Unfortunately, as Alvin fled from the cave, he dashed right across the pile of trash that had once been Larryboy. He kicked pieces of Larryboy in all directions.

"AHHHHHHHHH!" Phil screamed, running for a broom and dustpan. He wanted to sweep up all of the pieces of Larryboy before they got mixed up with other trash.

Meanwhile, as Alvin dashed out of the cave with

Lampy, followed by the chickens, he grabbed Vicki and took her prisoner. But Phil never noticed any of this because he was too busy sweeping up Larryboy.

"Larryboy! Speak to me!" Phil said to the trash.

"Hi, Phil. Thanks for bringing the chickens. It worked like a charm."

It was Larryboy's voice. Phil couldn't believe it. He looked closely at the pile of trash that he had just swept up. What he didn't see was Larryboy climbing out of the garbage can hanging upside down behind him.

"You can talk?" asked a shocked Phil, thinking that the little pieces of trash could speak.

"Of course I can talk. What were you expecting?"

"Don't worry, Larryboy! We'll figure out a way to put you back together."

Phil held the trash close to his face to see if he recognized Larryboy somewhere in the garbage.

"Nice garbage," Larryboy observed, looking over Phil's shoulder.

"These are pieces of Larryboy," Phil moaned, casting a glance over his shoulder. Then he did a double take.

"AHHHHHHHHH!" That was Phil screaming, in case you

hadn't already guessed.

"But how…?" Phil asked. "We saw—you were changed into trash!"

"Aw, that," said Larryboy. "Alvin's machine never changed me into garbage. His machine is powered by fear, but it didn't work on me, because I wouldn't let fear control me. Instead, I used my supersuction ears to hang onto the inside of the garbage can. When Alvin lifted the can back up, I was lifted up with it.

"I scraped some trash from the bottom of the can onto the ground—to confuse him," our hero added. "That's why he thought it was me. Pretty nifty, eh?" Larryboy glanced around. "Where's Vicki?"

Phil and Larryboy did a quick check of the room. Then they ran out of the cave and looked down the hill.

"**AHHHHHHHHH!**" This time, both Phil and Larryboy screamed at the same time. They could see, far down the hill, Alvin running away with Vicki as his prisoner, Lampy in tow.

"We've got to save her!" Phil shouted.

"I've got an idea," Larryboy said. "Would you grab that garbage can?"

"Sure thing!"

While Phil went to get the garbage can, Larryboy vanished into the bushes. Within seconds, he reemerged as Larry the Janitor.

"What happened to Larryboy?" asked a very confused Phil Winklesteen, when he came back with the garbage can.

"Larryboy asked me to take care of this personally," said Larry. "Have no fear." Then the brave janitor turned the can on its side and climbed into it. "Give me a little push, would you, Phil?"

Phil gave Larry a shove, and the silver garbage can went rolling and bouncing down the slope. Awful Alvin saw the garbage can coming, but he never stood a chance. The can hit a rock, bounced high into the air ... and barreled into Awful Alvin, like a bowling ball hitting a pin. Alvin went flying one direction and Lampy the other.

Phil came running down the slope, rope in hand. "Thought you might need this to tie up the loose ends," he said, handing the rope to Larry.

Before Alvin could regain his senses, Larry had the awful onion and his sidekick tied up like a sack of potatoes and sitting in the garbage can—ready for pickup by Officer Olaf.

CHAPTER 19

A NEW POWER

But the danger wasn't over yet.

Back in the heart of Bumblyburg, Gunkzilla broke loose from the cords that Larryboy had wrapped him in. The monster looked around for something to smash. His eyes (made out of cracked car headlights) locked onto the Burger Bell restaurant. Gunkzilla stomped in its direction, roaring every step of the way.

But that's when the monster began to slow down. Even his roar began to sound like a recording being played in slow motion. Gunkzilla was losing power.

The courage that Larryboy had shown back at the cave was having an effect on the Trash Reenergizer. As the machine sucked up Larryboy's courage, it began to sizzle, steam, rattle, and shake.

Other Veggies who had heard about the heroics also began to gain courage. Soon, bravery spread through Bumblyburg like a fresh wind. As the Trash Reenergizer sucked up this courage, it began to spark. Nuts and bolts holding the contraption together began to wiggle and pop out. The machine was having a complete breakdown. And then...

KABOOM!

The Trash Reenergizer went up in a fire-filled cloud of smoke.

But surprisingly, Gunkzilla didn't stop altogether. His eyes clicked on. His gears shifted. A new surge of energy moved through his trashy body. Gunkzilla was on the move again.

But there was a difference. Free from the power of the Trash Reenergizer, the monster began to clean up the mess he had made.

"Well, I'll be," said Officer Olaf with a big grin on his face. "The trash monster has become a giant garbage collector."

It was true. Gunkzilla tiptoed through the town, picking

up garbage and carrying it to the landfill. Bumblyburg was saved…and getting cleaner by the minute.

CHAPTER 20

SUPER JANITOR

As Bumblyburg returned to normal, Phil Winklesteen did one of the bravest things of his life. He told the people that he hadn't really saved those seven puppies from Bumbly Bay. He admitted that they had saved him.

To his surprise, the thing that he had feared most did not come to pass. The people of Bumblyburg didn't really care that he had been rescued by puppies. Instead, they were amazed by his and Larry the Janitor's courage in helping Larryboy defeat Alvin and Lampy. There was even some talk that his adventure would be made into a book.

As for Larry the Janitor and Vicki Cucumber...

"Larry, I couldn't believe how brave you were," Vicki said, as they headed back toward Bumblyburg. Then she stopped and looked down at the ground. "I'm sorry I got so angry with you the other day. I didn't know..."

"That's OK," Larry smiled.

"But I should've realized how brave you are, Larry. You were fearless!"

"Actually, I wasn't fearless," Larry said, as they continued on. "I was very scared. But Larryboy taught me that God wants us to do brave things even when we're scared silly."

Larry eyed Vicki's camera bag, which still had his letter sticking out of one of the pockets. "Uh...Vicki, did you ever read that letter from me?"

Vicki glanced down at the letter and blushed. "Oh...well, I'm afraid I didn't."

Larry breathed a big sigh of relief.

"I was so upset with you that I never even looked at it," she admitted. "But I'll read it right now."

"No, no, no, that's OK," said Larry, plucking the letter from her bag. "I said some things that I probably shouldn't have."

"I understand."

So Larry ripped up the letter and dropped it into the nearest trash can. Five minutes later, garbage men drove up in their truck, emptied the trash into the hopper, and rode off to the dump. The ripped-up letter wound up forty feet underground in the Bumblyburg Landfill.

Larryboy's secret was buried deep—where it belonged.

As for Awful Alvin...

He and Lampy were arrested on charges of "Assault with a Soggy Banana Peel." Then they were tossed into the Bumblyburg Pig-penitentiary, a prison for trashy criminals. Alvin spent long days plotting a way to escape and get his revenge on Larryboy.

When it was late at night and the darkness made him afraid, Alvin used his sidekick to light up his cell. Lampy was his own personal nightlight.

"We shall return," Alvin vowed, tucking himself into bed. "Good night, Lampy."

Alvin closed his eyes and began to count mutant sheep. "I'll get you, Larryboy," he muttered sleepily. "I'm not afraid of you...I'm not afraid..."

Suddenly, Lampy's lightbulb burned out and Alvin's cell became pitch dark.

"AHHHHHHHHHHHHHHHHHHHHHHHHHH!"

That was Awful Alvin, in case you hadn't already guessed.

THE END

VeggieTales®

LarryBoy™

VERSUS THE VOLCANO!

WRITTEN BY
DOUG PETERSON

ILLUSTRATED BY
MICHAEL MOORE

BASED ON THE HIT VIDEO SERIES: LARRYBOY
CREATED BY PHIL VISCHER
SERIES ADAPTED BY TOM BANCROFT

ZONDERkidz

ZONDERVAN.com/
AUTHORTRACKER
follow your favorite authors

TABLE OF CONTENTS

CHAPTER 1

A ROCKY BEGINNING

Larry the Cucumber

couldn't believe it was happening.

He was actually having a picnic with Vicki

Cucumber, the only girl to ever make his heart

skip a beat. For a mild-mannered janitor like

Larry, the day was postcard picture-perfect.

Larry and Vicki were on the grassy side of

Bumbly Mountain, which offered a great view of

Bumblyburg. There was only one glitch. Larry couldn't

come up with a thing to talk about.

"Um...did you know that a cockroach can live for

several weeks without its head?" asked Larry. He was

reading from his list of "Conversation Topics," prepared

especially for times like this.

"Uh...no, I didn't," Vicki answered.

Larry smiled and looked around nervously.

Then he snuck another peek at his Conversation Topics. "Did you know that houseflies like to—?"

"Maybe we should eat," Vicki suggested, quickly changing the subject.

"Good idea," agreed Larry, opening the picnic basket. He pulled out a chicken drumstick. "I made the chicken myself. It's an old family recipe that—"

"AHHHHHHHHHHHHHHHHHH!" Vicki suddenly screamed out of the blue.

Larry looked down at his chicken. "It doesn't taste that bad. You should just try it—"

"It's not the food!" Vicki yelled. "It's *that!*"

Larry looked up the hill. A giant boulder had cracked loose from the side of the mountain and was heading right toward them.

With swift, cucumber reflexes, Larry shoved Vicki out of the way. But he didn't have time to save himself. The rock was upon him!

"Larry!" shouted Vicki, closing her eyes. She couldn't look as Larry the Cucumber was about to become squash.

Larry flipped forward on top of the rock as it raced downhill. But his troubles were just beginning. Trying to stay on top of a rolling stone was like running on a very dangerous treadmill. Larry rode the boulder as it barreled down the mountain at breakneck speed—emphasis on breaking necks.

The boulder was headed straight for Bumbly Park, which was packed with Veggies attending the annual Taste of Bumblyburg Celebration. The crowd was an easy target for an out-of-control boulder.

When the rock came upon a small ledge, it went flying, flipping Larry high into the air. The rock crashed back down onto the ground with a **THUD** that shook the mountain like a dinosaur's step.

Larry also hit the ground with an **"OOF!"** and began to roll downhill, out of control. He somersaulted down the side of the mountain, over and over and over.

Kind of like a boulder, come to think of it.

The chase was on.

CHAPTER 2

BETWEEN A ROCK AND A HARD PLACE

Screaming Veggies scattered like ants as the big boulder smashed its way through Bumbly Park. The boulder pulverized a taco stand, flattened a hot dog cart, and headed straight for a group of innocent and unsuspecting Cub Sprouts!

Fortunately, Larry had recently taken a special training course on how to switch into his superhero costume while swimming, skydiving, playing hop-scotch, and...amazingly...while rolling down a hill totally out of control. By the time Larry the Janitor had rolled through the crowd in Bumbly Park, he had changed into Bumblyburg's most famous, most purplish hero of all time...LARRYBOY!

"I AM THAT HERO!" he shouted, firing one of his supersuction ears.

THONK!

The plunger hit the boulder and held fast. Larryboy was sure that the tether cord stretching from the plunger back to his head would be enough to stop the boulder. But he underestimated the power of the rock. The boulder yanked Larryboy up into the air.

The rock closed in on the Cub Sprouts, who were now frozen with fear.

Meanwhile, Larryboy's tether cord wrapped 'round and 'round the rolling boulder as Larryboy flew behind in midair, being pulled in closer and closer to the boulder—like string around a ball.

ZIP!

Larryboy sent a second supersuction ear zipping toward the side of a nearby bagel truck. **THONK!** The purple protector anchored himself to the side of the truck, hoping to slow the rampaging boulder on the other side.

Only one problem...

Larryboy felt like he was being torn apart between the rock and the bagel truck! As the truck tipped back on its rear wheels, the doors swung open and thousands of bagels came rolling out.

But the cords held fast, finally bringing the boulder to a stop...just inches before crushing the Cub Sprouts.

As the crowd dodged different flavored bagels, they let out a cheer, and Larryboy smiled in relief.

"Thank you, thank you, it was nothing," our hero said, pulling out a chicken drumstick, which had become caught in his cape while he changed into his costume.

"**AHHHHHHHHHHHHHHH!**" the people screamed.

"What is it about my chicken that causes such a reaction?" Larryboy asked, staring at his drumstick.

"It's not the chicken, Larryboy!" shouted Officer Olaf.

"It's that!"

Larryboy spun around and looked right into the angry eyes of the boulder! "*Eyes?*" said Larryboy. "Since when do boulders have eyes?"

"I not only have eyes," spoke the rock. "I also have a mouth."

With that, the boulder laughed and breathed out the worst stream of bad breath that Larryboy had ever whiffed. The rock's breath was burning hot and spicy, with just a hint of dog breath, dirty gym socks, and unwashed weasel smell.

In fact, the odor was so powerful that Larryboy fell over backwards, completely unconscious.

With Larryboy out of the picture, the rock let loose another evil laugh that would have scored high in the annual Villainous Laugh Contest at the Bumblyburg State Fair. Then the rock rolled right through the side of the Scuba-Tuba Superstore—the largest store in the world devoted to underwater diving equipment and tubas.

"Let's rock and roll!" laughed the rock, stealing scuba gear right and left.

But Larryboy wasn't defeated yet. The wobbly super-hero regained consciousness and spotted the boulder driving a forklift that loaded scuba gear onto a truck.

"Yo, Rocky! Release that scuba gear!" Larryboy shouted, trying to strike a dramatic pose (which was hard to do while dazed and dizzy).

The boulder wheeled around in surprise. "So the pickle boy woke up! You know what you get when you wake up, don't you? DRAGON BREATH!" The boulder smiled wickedly and breathed another mouthful of deadly odors.

The last thing Larryboy remembered smelling was a mixture of superheated air, tangy spices, and spoiled milk. Then everything went dark.

CHAPTER 3

GETTING AWAY FROM IT ALL

"It's a good thing

you have a spare costume. This one

may be ruined," said Archibald, Larryboy's

faithful servant.

Archie was trying to scrub the foul smell

from Larryboy's costume, while our cucumber hero

lounged around in his bathrobe, sipping Slushees.

It was nighttime, and Larryboy was back inside the

Larrycave.

"By the way, what did that rocky rascal get away

with?" Larryboy asked sleepily.

"He stole every piece of scuba and snorkeling gear

in the store, Master Larry."

"Scuba gear?" Larryboy asked, puzzled. "What

would a rock do with scuba gear?"

"I'm not certain. First, tell me about your time

with Vicki. Were you enjoying yourselves before the boulder hit the scene?"

Larryboy's eyes lit up. "Vicki and I had a great time, Archie. I just wish I didn't always have to save Bumblyburg so often—and at the worst of times! It's exhausting." Larryboy took another sip of his chocolate mocha-mint vanilla swirl frozen drink.

"I see," said Archie, madly scrubbing the Larryboy costume.

"I've been thinking that I could use a vacation," Larryboy said, sinking deeper into his cushy couch. "I need time off when I can't be interrupted."

"A vacation would be nice," Archie agreed, scrubbing even harder.

Larryboy sprang from the couch. "I'm glad you agree! I know just the place to go." He unfolded a large, colorful brochure. "It's called Superhero Island!"

Archie set aside the soggy costume, took the brochure, and sat down to read it. "Where did you get this, Master Larry?"

"Someone stuck it on the windshield of the Larrymobile. Doesn't Superhero Island sound great? Beautiful beaches! Scuba diving! Gourmet dining!"

Archie continued to read:

TIRED OF LEAPING TALL BUILDINGS
OR RUNNING FASTER THAN A SPEEDING LOCOMOTIVE?
DO ORDINARY PEOPLE EXPECT YOU TO SAVE THE WORLD,
EVEN IN THE MIDDLE OF YOUR FAVORITE CARTOON?
YOU DESERVE A BREAK TODAY ON
SUPERHERO ISLAND!

YOU'LL BE SURROUNDED BY THE **GREATEST,**
MOST HEROIC, AND **IMPORTANT**
PEOPLE ON THE PLANET—OTHER SUPERHEROES!
SUPERHERO ISLAND IS AN EXCLUSIVE RESORT,
SPECIALLY CREATED FOR **SUPER PEOPLE ONLY.**

IMAGINE:
AN ENTIRE WEEK WITH
THE BEST OF THE BEST!
YOU'LL HAVE A PERFECT TIME WHEN
YOU'RE WITH **PERFECT** PEOPLE!

"It sounds a little snooty to me," said Archie.

"Oh, don't be a stick-in-the-mud," laughed Larryboy.

Archie shook his head. "Well…if this is where you

really want to go for vacation, I'll pack the bags."

"Superhero Island, here we come!"

CHAPTER 4

TURNING UP THE HEAT

A thousand miles away from the Larrycave was a cave of a completely different sort. This was a dark, secluded cave, tucked away on a deserted jungle island. Torches and multicolored lava lamps eerily lit up the cave.

This was none other than the secret hideout of the world-famous Chili Pepper. However, Chili Pepper was not world-famous for being a supervillain, as you're probably thinking. No one even knew about Chili's wicked ways. Instead, Chili Pepper was famous for being "the Snooty Gourmet," a television chef who gave tips on how to make chili a hundred different ways.

Chili's sidekick was Coconut, a muscular thug who dreamed of someday becoming much more than just a sidekick. He wanted to be a supervillain himself. In fact, he was taking an evil genius correspondence course and was busily doing his homework.

"Um, Chili Pepper, what do you think about this question?" Coconut said, holding up his quiz. "Question 4 says: 'If you had evil mutant power, what would you use it for? (A) To take over the world; (B) To wreak havoc and destruction; or (C) To floss regularly?' I was thinking the answer might be D."

"D? There is no D," said Chili Pepper.

"I know. But I think this is a trick question. D is an invisible answer. They put it in just to fool me."

"Ah...good thinking," said Chili Pepper, rolling his eyes. "Then maybe you should fill out all of your answers in invisible ink."

"Great idea!" grinned Coconut.

Chili Pepper stood at his deluxe stove, testing his latest chili recipe. He was famous for making the hottest, spiciest chili in the universe—chili so spicy that it brought tears to your eyes from a block away.

"By the way, Coconut, how many superheroes have signed up to come to our island retreat?" Chili Pepper asked, tasting his hot concoction.

Coconut set aside his quiz to check the registration

book. "One hundred and thirty-five superheroes are coming to Superhero Island, boss. That's a lot of spandex!"

"That's almost every superhero in the world," snickered Chili Pepper. "Little do they know that Superhero Island is really a Tourist Trap! Emphasis on the word 'trap'!"

"Good one, Boss!" Coconut laughed. Then his smile vanished as a thought crossed his mind—a rare event. "But what about this mysterious volcanic rock I've heard about? Do you think this creature will be mad when it finds out what we're doing to the island's volcano? Personally, that rock scares me."

"Don't worry about a piece of stone," said Chili Pepper, stirring the chili. "Let's concentrate on the superheroes. They don't realize that I've cooked up one big surprise for them. When they arrive, they're going to get a taste of my awesome power!"

Chili Pepper's laugh echoed through the caves, rumbling ominously throughout the entire island.

CHAPTER 5

AN INVITATION TO DANGER

Larry the Janitor had never seen Bob the Tomato this way before. Bob had always been the super-serious, hardworking editor of the *Daily Bumble* newspaper.

But not today.

Today, Bob the Tomato was wearing a Hawaiian shirt, a big straw hat, and sunglasses. Polynesian music floated out of Bob's office as Larry the Janitor prepared to mop his floor.

"What's up?" Larry asked.

"I'll tell you what's up!" Bob exclaimed, taking Larry's mop and dancing around the room with it.

"I'm going on the assignment of a lifetime! I'm off to Superhero Island!"

Larry almost blurted out, "So am I!" But he

caught himself just in time. You see, no one but Archie knew that Larry was much more than a mild-mannered janitor for the *Daily Bumble*. No one else knew that he was also LARRYBOY!

"That's nice," he said instead.

"Vicki and I have been invited to Superhero Island to do an exclusive report on this new resort for superheroes," Bob explained, popping open his luggage and checking to make sure he had everything. "I'm doing the story, and Vicki is taking photos. Even though it's work, it'll feel like a vacation."

"Well, don't forget your sunblock," Larry said, pulling a tube out of Bob's suitcase and handing it to him. "You're already looking pretty red."

"I'm a tomato, Larry. Tomatoes *are* red!"

"Oh. Right."

"This is going to be the most fun assignment ever!" Bob shouted as he spread the sunscreen on his face. "Hey! This is minty-smelling sunscreen. I like it!"

Larry took a closer look at the tube that he had just handed to Bob. Then he quickly ducked out of the room as he spotted Vicki about to enter Bob's office.

"How come you smeared toothpaste all over your face,

Chief?" Vicki asked as she entered the room.

As Larry hopped onto the elevator, he heard Bob shout, "LARRY!"

So much for Bob's good mood. He quickly pushed the "down" button.

CHAPTER 6
VACATION FEVER

You probably know what it's like on the last day of school before vacation. Well, that's pretty much what it was like in Larryboy's Superhero 101 class later that day at Bumblyburg Community College.

Most of the superheroes didn't have their minds on their studies or their eyes on their instructor, Bok Choy. Their eyes were on the clock, and their minds were on Superhero Island. Almost every superhero in the class was planning to go on vacation to the island.

The Scarlet Tomato sat in class wearing snorkeling gear. Electro-Melon had stuffed a surfboard into his school backpack. And Larryboy was blowing up a huge, inflatable rubber ducky.

Each hero had received the same Superhero Island brochure. And each one of them was convinced they were the BEST OF THE BEST and wanted the perfect getaway with perfect people.

Each superhero's pride inflated just as rapidly as the rubber ducky that Larryboy was blowing up.

"Larryboy, I hate to take the air out of your duck, but would you read today's lesson from the Superhero Handbook?" said Bok Choy.

"Mmmm?" Larryboy asked, his mouth still puffing on the slowly inflating raft.

"Please read Section 45, paragraph 12, line 16 in your Superhero Handbook."

"MMMMMMM MMMMM MM MMMMMM MMM MMMM," Larryboy mumbled, reading from the Handbook.

"Perhaps you could stop inflating your raft while you read," Bok Choy suggested.

Larryboy let out a big sigh, reluctantly releasing his mouth from the duck's blower-upper thingie. Instantly, all of the air gushed out, and the duck took off like a balloon rocket.

"DUCK!"

The deflating duck flew wildly around the room, bouncing off walls, knocking over the globe, swooping around Electro-Melon's surfboard, crashing into a stack of books, and finally winding up on top of Bok Choy's desk.

"Oops," said Larryboy.

"Please proceed," urged Bok Choy patiently.

Larryboy stood up and read: "Don't be proud. Be willing to be a friend of people who aren't considered important. Don't think that you are better than others."

"Very good, Larryboy," said their wise instructor. "As the Handbook says, when we think we're better than others, we become proud and arrogant. And when we're arrogant, we don't want to be seen with people we think are unimportant. We exclude them and don't treat them as God wants us to."

Bok Choy paused because no one was paying attention. Every superhero was watching the clock, counting the seconds to when the bell would ring. So Bok Choy yanked the clock off the wall and hung it around his neck like a giant medallion. That way, at least the students would be looking in his direction.

He continued, "When we exclude others, we become filled with even more pride and arrogance. So remember that EVERYONE is important in God's eyes. As superheroes, you should set an example of this."

Bok Choy stopped and sighed. "Did any of you hear one word I said?"

Nope. Every eye was waiting for the second hand on the clock to make one final sweep. 5-4-3-2-1...

RINNNNNNNNGGGGG!

The bell had rung. Class was over.

"Vacation time!"

Like a stampede of crazed water buffaloes, the entire class stormed out of the room. If Bok Choy hadn't done his famous ninja triple flip into the air, he might have been trampled to the ground. Instead, he wound up safely on top of his desk, nestled securely inside Larryboy's rubber duck.

"I know exactly how you feel," he said to the duck. "After a class like today, I'm pretty deflated, too."

CHAPTER 7

SECOND-CLASS CITIZENS

Chili Pepper and his sidekick, Coconut, stood on the edge of the Superhero Island runway, watching superhero after superhero arrive by supersonic jet, atomic-powered helicopter, or rocket backpack. Larryboy swooped in on his Larryplane.

"De plane! De plane!" Coconut shouted as each plane hit the runway. "De plane! De plane! De—"

"Coconut, knock it off," Chili Pepper said.

"Sorry, Boss. But I always wanted to say that."

As Larryboy and Archie hopped out of the cockpit, several island girls rushed up to take their luggage, hand them a glass of lemonade, and welcome them to Superhero Island. Each girl wore a sticker that said, "HELLO, My name is _____. I'm not as important as *you.*"

"Didn't I tell you this would be great?" said Larryboy. "I feel relaxed already!"

"I'm glad *someone's* relaxed," said Archibald. He wasn't feeling very comfortable disguised as Larryboy's airplane mechanic, wearing bib overalls, a bandana, and grease streaked across his face—probably the only mechanic to wear a monocle.

The island was paradise—the thick rain forest was overrun with monkeys and colorful birds. The water was clear, the waterfalls plentiful, and beautiful streams cut across the landscape from a huge, majestic mountain in the center of the island.

"That's Mount Superhero," announced Chili Pepper, as he and Coconut welcomed their guests.

"And that's Chili Pepper, the Snooty Gourmet," whispered Larryboy to Archie. "I watch his cooking show on TV all the time. If he's running things, the food's gonna be great! Chili-filled donuts...chili pancakes...chili chocolate cake...!"

"He must like his chili hot and spicy," noted Archie, as Chili Pepper tossed a breath mint into his mouth. "His breath could peel wallpaper."

Everything on the island was picture-perfect postcard.

Except for one slight hitch.

As the superheroes lined up to enter the resort, Chili Pepper asked each one of them a question.

"What makes you a superhero?" Chili asked Larryboy's friend Lemon Twist.

"At an early age, I discovered that I had the ability to control the air within a one-foot radius around my body," Lemon Twist said. "I can create gale-force winds."

"Nice, very nice," said Chili Pepper. "You may enter."

Lemon Twist hopped forward, and a robotic arm shot out from the wall, planting an invisible stamp smack in the center of her forehead.

As each superhero entered the resort, it was always the same question. "What makes you a superhero?"

Unfortunately, some didn't make the cut.

"My super power is shooting straw wrappers for distances up to a half mile using a highly refined laser guidance system," said a lima bean who called himself Straw Man.

Chili Pepper scoffed. "You call that a superhero power? Sorry, you're not important enough. Go home."

In desperation, Straw Man pulled out one of his laser-guided straws. But before he could fire off a single wrapper, a robotic foot came out of the wall and booted Straw Man out of line.

"Some people have all the nerve," Larryboy whispered to Archie. "They think they're an important superhero when they're NOT. Party crashers."

"And what makes you a superhero?" Chili Pepper asked when Larryboy finally reached the front of the line.

"My supersuction ears!" Larryboy declared proudly, his cape flapping in the breeze. "I even have my own line of action figures. I AM THAT HERO!"

"But what is your super power?" Chili Pepper asked.

Larryboy was stunned. "Super power? Well..."

"Some superheroes don't have special powers," Archie chimed in. "Instead, Larryboy uses amazing gadgets and vehicles, such as the Larryplane and the Larrymobile. I should know. I work on them. See the grease?"

"I've protected Bumblyburg from dastardly villains for years," Larryboy added, panic rising. "You can't exclude me from the island!"

"Calm down," said Chili Pepper. "You can stay on the island, but I'm afraid you won't be included in the First Class section of our exclusive resort. Because you don't have special powers, you and your mechanic will have to stay in the Second Class section."

Larryboy let out a big sigh of relief. "Second Class section. I can live with that. That's not so bad. That's—"

Suddenly, the robotic boot gave both Larryboy and Archie a big wallop. Kicked high in the air, the caped cucumber and his mechanic landed head-first in the sand—right in front of the Second Class entrance.

Larryboy popped his head out of the sand and looked at the gate to the Second Class section. The gate was falling off of its rusty hinges.

"Carry yer own luggage," snapped a snooty servant, walking by with his nose in the air.

"Are we having fun yet?" Archie asked, spitting sand from his mouth.

CHAPTER 8

RECIPE FOR DISASTER

Later that night, Coconut was going nuts. Freaking out. He dashed into their secret cave hideout, only to find Chili Pepper calmly cooking another gigantic pot of chili.

"What is it now, big guy?" Chili asked, rolling his eyes.

"That rock! He's here. On the island. I saw a rock, and it stared at me with EYES! It was really creepy!"

"So what's the big deal?" asked Chili Pepper.

"That volcanic rock is going to be furious when he finds out what we're doing to the island's volcano!"

"You worry too much, Coconut. It's not good for your digestion. Now read that recipe back to me."

Although Chili Pepper liked hot food, he was one cool customer.

"Which recipe?" Coconut said, flipping through the Evil Genius Cookbook.

"You know, the recipe for my greatest culinary creation of all time: Volcano Chili!"

"Oh. Right. Here it is," said Coconut. "First step: Fill the inside of a volcano with 23 zillion gallons of chili. Stir vigorously."

"Done," said Chili Pepper.

"Second step: Add 14 trillion pounds of shredded cheese."

"Done."

"Third," continued Coconut, "while the chili simmers, bake 33 billion giant dinner rolls, then add them to the volcanic mixture."

"That's also been done."

"Turn on the invisible force field to trap everyone on the island."

"Check," said Chili Pepper.

"Make sure your escape pod is ready," read Coconut.

"Done."

"Finally, bring chili to a boil, then trigger several underground explosions. A volcanic eruption should occur within an hour. Serves 135."

"Aha! Setting the timer for an explosion is the only thing left for us to do," said Chili Pepper, pushing a button on a remote-control device.

WHIRRRRRRR...KA-CHUNK!

That was the sound of an entire cave wall sliding open to reveal what looked like the largest pop can ever created. The can was as big as a house, and it contained Chili Pepper's personal brand of pop—Chili-Cola, a spicy, chili-flavored soft drink.

"That's one big can," said Coconut. "What's it got to do with explosions?"

"Watch and learn," said Chili. He pushed another button, and a huge mechanical hand shot out of the wall. It grabbed the monstrous can and began to shake...and shake...and shake.

"**OOOOOOOOOOO**, I get it," said Coconut. "Shake this can, and it explodes when you open it."

"That's right," laughed Chili Pepper villainously. "We're going to let this can shake all day. When the top is popped tomorrow, this carbonated time bomb is going to fizz and explode, setting off a chain reaction. The exploding pop can will trigger earthquakes, causing the volcano to blow, which will destroy the entire island! Every superhero here will be trapped as the island slowly sinks into the sea."

Coconut and Chili Pepper clambered up a spiral staircase that ran alongside the monstrous pop can.

"What should I set it for, Boss?" Coconut asked, peering at the timer on the shaking machine.

"Fourteen hours should give us plenty of time. We've got to make our guests feel at home…before they're blown to bits."

The countdown began. The island had become a giant, ticking time bomb, ready to pop its top.

By the following morning, disaster would be served.

CHAPTER 9

BEACH BUMMER

The next day, Bob and Vicki found Larryboy and Archie on the Second Class beach, trying to catch a little sun.

While Vicki snapped photos, Bob pulled out his notebook and peppered Larryboy with questions. "So how's everything on the Second Class side?"

"Is this on the record?" Larryboy asked.

Bob nodded.

"Well, I'm glad you asked, Bob! Things are LOUSY on the Second Class side of the island. Service is horrible! The dinners come out of vending machines. And there are no maids to clean up the rooms."

"He's correct," added Archie. "So many things on this side of the island are broken that a roll of duct tape is left in every room, right next to the Standard Superhero Handbook (which is also taped together)."

Even the Second Class beach was a mess. The sand was covered with little burrs that stuck to your body. And every beach chair was patched together with...what else? Duct tape.

But that wasn't the worst of it.

"HOWDY! HOWDY! HOWDY! My name is Tourist-Man!"

That was the worst of it.

Tourist-Man was a carrot whose super power was his ability to put people to sleep with his boring vacation pictures. He wore a bright Hawaiian shirt, lugged around three huge pieces of luggage filled with photo albums and vacation slides, and spoke so loudly that you wished he had a mute button.

"SAY CHEESE!" yelled Tourist-Man obnoxiously.

FLASH!

Did I mention that he also carried around a camera and took flash pictures in your face approximately every five seconds?

"I guess I'll be on the Second Class side of the beach from now on!" Tourist-Man shouted, setting up his slide projector right there on the beach. "I just got voted off of the other side of the island. CAN YOU BELIEVE IT?"

"I can't imagine why," said Bob sarcastically.

"Say, I like your camera!" Tourist-Man noted, when he spotted Vicki's camera equipment. "Does it have a flash as bright as mine? SAY CHEESE!"

FLASH!

Vicki staggered backwards as the light left her seeing spots. "You can get sunburn from a flash that bright," she said, running into a nearby palm tree.

"Isn't it great?" beamed Tourist-Man.

Quietly escaping Tourist-Man's chaotic presence, Larryboy wandered over to the huge privacy wall that separated the First Class side from the Second Class side of the beach. The voices of happy, laughing superheroes on the other side infuriated him. He felt terribly left out.

"THAT'S IT!" Larryboy scowled. "I'm not taking this any more! I'm going over the wall!"

With that, the caped cucumber climbed up the wall and squeezed beneath the barbed wire top. Then he leaped onto the First Class side of the beach...

...and found himself in a whole new world.

CHAPTER 10

THE SUPER SNUB

On the First Class side, the beach was as white as snow. Not a burr in sight. Servants swarmed everywhere, serving every superhero's desire. The First Class superheroes also had their pick of jet skis, motorboats, sailboats, scuba gear, and even jet packs.

Larryboy tried to blend in with the First Class crowd but was immediately spotted.

"What ya'll doing here, Larryboy?" asked Sweet Potato, a down-home Southern superhero who happened to be as strong as a Mack Truck.

"Sssshhhhh, I'm just hanging out," whispered Larryboy.

"Hey, Larryboy, what's up?" asked Lemon Twist. "Aren't you

supposed to be on the Second Class side? Or have you developed special powers in the past day?"

The Scarlet Tomato, following just behind Lemon Twist, chuckled. "I don't-a think Chili Pepper will be happy if he sees-a you here. This side is-a for the more important superheroes, you know."

"You don't believe that, do you?" Larryboy said.

"Well, it does make some sense," said Sweet Potato. "I mean, if ya'll didn't have your contraptions, you wouldn't be much of a superhero, would you, sweet thing? We're superheroes, with or without contraptions. That makes us more important."

"As my uncle Guido would-a say, 'If you-a got it, you-a got it.' And we-a got it," said the Scarlet Tomato.

"What seems to be the trouble here?" boomed a loud voice from directly behind Larryboy. It was Coconut, the bouncer.

Coconut took one look at Larryboy and nearly split his shell. "WHAT are you doing on the First Class side of the beach, pickle boy?"

"It's really very simple..."

"Save your breath, gadget guy!" said Coconut as he hurled Larryboy up and over the wall.

Back on the Second Class side of the beach, Bob, Vicki, Archie, and Tourist-Man watched as Larryboy came sailing over the wall, landing headfirst in the sand.

"SAY CHEESE!" Tourist-Man exclaimed, clicking photos of Larryboy upside down in the sand.

FLASH!

Larryboy felt rejected and all-around lousy...until he realized there was something under the sand where he landed.

"This is strange," he said—although with his head in the sand it sounded more like, **"MMMM MM MMMMMMM."**

Archie helped Larryboy out of the sand. Larryboy repeated himself. "Guys! There's something here!"

As the group gathered around, Larryboy used the toy beach shovel on his utility belt to dig wildly in the sand. About a foot below the surface, he uncovered a metal trapdoor.

"I bet I know what *that* is," Larryboy said. "It's a secret passageway to the First Class side of the beach."

Bob whistled softly. "You could be right."

"I'll check it out."

The caped cucumber yanked open the hatch and leaped in—which was not a good move. He should have looked before he leaped.

"*Yikes!*"

Yikes was right. Larryboy found himself tumbling toward a stream of very hot liquid. And if he wasn't mistaken, it looked an awful lot like lava. Red-hot lava. Volcanic lava.

"ARCHIE! HEEEEEEEEELP!"

CHAPTER 11

THE TIME BOMB

Larryboy fired off both of his supersuction ears. The first suction cup hit a slippery stalactite in the underground cave but didn't catch hold. (Stalactites are those pointy rocks that hang down from cave ceilings like fangs.) The second plunger caught the cave's ceiling just in time, preventing Larryboy from taking a very hot lava bath. The caped cucumber dangled upside down from the tether cord, only inches above the thick, steaming liquid. "SAY CHEESE!" called Tourist-Man from the trapdoor above.

FLASH!

"Excuse me, Tourist-Man," said Archie, bumping the carrot aside as he peeked down into the cave. "Are you all right, Larryboy? What's down there?"

"Well…at first I thought it was lava," said Larryboy. "But after I took a couple of sniffs, I think it smells an awful lot like chili."

Larryboy stuck out his tongue and took a taste. "Mmmmmmmm, tastes like chili!" He took another slurp.

"Easy, Larryboy, you've already had four bowls of Chili Crunch cereal this morning," said Archie. "You don't want to spend the rest of this adventure in the bathroom."

"Good point. Do you suppose Chili Pepper is behind all of this chili?" Larryboy asked.

"Most likely," said Archie. "But I'm not sure why."

"There's a ladder leading down here. Why don't you climb down and help me find some clues!" Larryboy called. "There's also a path alongside this stream."

Archie, Bob, and Vicki clambered down the ladder and released Larryboy from the ceiling. Tourist-Man wasn't far behind, groaning as he dragged along his three giant pieces of luggage and his camera.

"Do you have to carry luggage everywhere you go?" Vicki asked.

"Wouldn't be caught dead without it," said Tourist-Man, wheeling around and nearly knocking Bob into the chili-lava with one of his suitcases. Larryboy caught Bob

just in time by using a supersuction ear.

"Let's follow the cave's trail," said Vicki.

So the adventurers took off, bouncing along the underground pathway. The stream of chili-lava bubbled and
steamed, making the tunnel as hot as a sauna. Along the
trail, the heroes didn't even need a flashlight because
Tourist-Man's nonstop flashing went off every few seconds,
providing plenty of illumination.

"What in the world...?" gasped Bob. The little group
came across a second stream. Only this was a stream of
melted cheese. The cheese merged with the chili, creating
one great big gurgling river of molten food.

"SAY CHEESE!" Tourist-Man bellowed. "Get it? Say cheese?"

Larryboy found another ladder, which led to an upper level lit by torches. The group marched through two large rooms until they came across the most shocking sight of all. A large mechanical hand was wildly shaking a monstrous pop can.

"Chili-Cola," smiled Larryboy. "My favorite."

"But why the mega pop can?" asked Bob. "What's it for?"

Archie climbed the spiral staircase alongside the giant pop can, studying the shaking contraption every step of the way. "I hate to say this," said Archie. "But this is a Fizz Bomb. The pop can is set to open in approximately one hour."

"You mean...?" gasped Bob.

"Yes. When the mechanical hand opens, this pop can is going to explode!"

"But why?" asked Vicki.

"It's probably set to trigger an earthquake or volcanic eruption," said Archie.

"Earthquakes! Volcanoes! Finally, I'm going to have a vacation slide show that won't put people to sleep," grinned Tourist-Man.

Larryboy hopped up beside Archie. "Is there any way we can disconnect the pop can before it explodes?"

"Sure there is," said Archie. "By cutting the wire on the machine...the correct wire."

Archie nodded toward a tangle of wires, which led from the timer to the shaking device.

"The big question is," paused Archie, "do we cut the red wire? Or do we cut the blue one?"

"What happens if we cut the wrong one?" asked Vicki.

"KA-BOOM!" shouted Tourist-Man happily.

"That would be an accurate conclusion," Archie stated.

CHAPTER 12

SAY CHEESE!

Larryboy removed a pair of wire cutters from his utility belt and handed them to Archie.

"Thanks," said Archie, although he didn't say it with much enthusiasm.

"Do you have any idea which wire to cut?" Vicki asked.

"Not a clue."

"I once saw a TV movie where two guys were trying to figure out which wire to cut," offered Larryboy. "The star of the show cut the red wire and that defused the bomb."

Archie started to cut the red wire.

"NO, WAIT!" Larryboy shouted just in

time to stop him. "I just remembered. The colors on my TV were messed up that day. I think the red wire was really blue. They cut the BLUE wire to defuse the bomb."

Archie started to cut the blue wire.

"NO, WAIT!" Larryboy shouted just in time. "Actually, I had my TV repaired on the morning that I saw the movie. I think the red wire was red after all. Cut the red wire."

Archie started to cut the red wire.

"NO, WAIT!" Larryboy shouted. "I just remembered. The TV I owned at that time was a black-and-white set. Very retro. I have no idea which color wire the hero cut."

"I once heard that villains always use blue wires to detonate their bombs," interjected Tourist-Man. "That way, they always remember which wire sets off an explosion. Blue causes **KA-BLOOEY**. Get it?"

Sighing, Archie began to cut the blue wire.

As Archie paused for one terrifying moment before he snipped the wire, Tourist-Man exclaimed, "I've got to get this historic event on film. SAY CHEESE!"

FLASH!

The flash burst in Archie's face at the precise moment when the asparagus was cutting the blue wire.

The result?

Well, let's just say that Archie's wire cutters slipped a little.

Okay, they slipped A LOT.

Archie accidentally cut BOTH WIRES!

"This is not good," he said.

Everyone took a quick look at the timer to see what would happen. The clock had changed! Instead of one hour before the pop-can explosion, the timer switched to five seconds.

Five measly seconds.

CHAPTER 13

5...4...3...2...1...

Pop!

FIZZZZZZZZZZZZZZZZZZZZ
ZZZZZZZZZZZZZ!

KA-
BLOOEY!

CHAPTER 14

VOLCANIC VILLAINY

A lot of the First Class superheroes were innocently frolicking on the beach when the underground explosion rocked the island. The pop-can explosion set off small earthquakes and created large waves.

Sweet Potato was about to take a bite of her cotton candy when the ground suddenly lurched.

She stumbled face-first into her cotton candy, couldn't see where she was going, and fell onto American Pie's lawn chair.

American Pie was catapulted out into the water, where he knocked Lemon Twist off of her surf-board.

Lemon Twist landed on top of the Scarlet Tomato, who was trying to drive a jet ski.

Blinded, the Scarlet Tomato ran his jet ski up on the beach, destroying Electro-Melon's sand castle.

Electro-Melon dove out of the way, landing on the end of a large table covered with cake, chips, punch, little hot dogs, and all kinds of silverware.

About a hundred dessert forks shot up into the air like silver arrows and rained down on a stack of inflatable inner tubes.

The inner tubes popped and shot all over the place, while people screamed, fell, and tried to dodge falling chunks of cake.

You get the idea.

Meanwhile, on the opposite side of the island, in a deserted cove, Coconut stood all alone on a beach. His escape pod was anchored in the water, a short distance away. Like everyone else, Coconut had felt the force of the underground explosion.

"What in the world?" he said. "The pop can wasn't supposed to explode for another hour."

Looking at the tip-top of Mount Superhero, Coconut saw a black cloud of smoke pour from the crater like a genie from a bottle. The volcano hadn't erupted yet, but it wouldn't be long before the mountain blew its lid.

"Where's Chili Pepper?" Coconut fretted. "He was supposed to be here a half hour ago! We need to get off this island. Fast!"

At that moment, a giant rock came hurtling toward Coconut like a meteor. Spotting it just in time, Coconut rolled to the side as the rock crashed into the sand.

"Whew! That was a close one," Coconut said, leaning against the rock and wiping his forehead with a handkerchief.

He didn't notice as the rock slowly opened two eyes— two very *angry* eyes.

"What are ya doing messin' with my volcano?" snarled the volcanic rock.

At the sound of the rock's voice, Coconut leaped ten feet forward and spun around. "I...We...I...didn't know it was your volcano."

"Well, now you know," said the rock. "You can tell your little chili friend the same thing." The rock skipped across the water and hopped into the cockpit of Chili Pepper's escape pod.

"Hey, you can't take that submarine! That's ours!" Coconut made a mad dash toward the boulder, but the rock monster sent out a blistering stream of bad breath, knocking Coconut backwards.

Revving the engine, the mysterious rock steered the escape pod into deeper water, then disappeared under the surface, leaving behind only a cloud of bubbles—and one very confused Coconut.

CHAPTER 15

SURF'S UP, DUDE!

Back in the underground

tunnels...

When the pop can opened, a huge stream

of Chili-Cola exploded from the earth, hitting

Veggies like water from a fire hose and hurling

them backwards. But because Chili-Cola is cold and

refreshing, the Veggies survived the drenching. They

simply felt...sticky...

...and very angry...at Tourist-Man.

"Will you knock it off with the pictures!" Bob

shouted, furious that Tourist-Man's incessant flash had

caused Archie to cut both wires.

"No wonder you were voted off the other side

of the island!" Vicki snapped. "Look what you've

done!"

"Maybe we should vote on whether Tourist-Man gets to stay on our side of the island," suggested Larryboy.

"Don't you think you're being a bit harsh, Master Larry?" Archie asked.

"Anyone who wants me off the island, raise your hand," Tourist-Man offered, glancing around. "OK, no hands—I stay."

"Very funny," said Bob. "We don't have hands. Let's vote on paper."

Bob tore pieces of paper from his notebook and passed them around for the vote. It was unanimous. Tourist-Man was booted from the Second Class side of the island. He was stunned, speechless. For the first time since they had met him, his big grin had vanished. "You're kicking me off this side of the island, too?"

"I guess we are. Sorry. It's a matter of survival."

Tourist-Man's face wore the saddest expression they had ever seen. Piling his three giant pieces of luggage on his back, Tourist-Man slowly turned and trudged away. A couple of times, he paused to throw a sad look over his shoulder.

The group could hear him sniff as he wandered off in the opposite direction.

"Gee. Maybe we were a little too hard on him," Larryboy said after Tourist-Man had disappeared into a tunnel.

"Yes, I believe we may have been," said Archie. "Maybe we—"

But there was no time for regrets now. A heavy-duty earthquake suddenly rose up from the depths of the cave, knocking everyone to the ground. Cracks opened up in the cave floor and spread like fast-growing, flaming fingers. Red-hot chili spurted and bubbled through the cracks, flooding the tunnel with extra-spicy chili sauce!

Bob, Archie, Larryboy, and Vicki could hear the roar of something approaching them from the tunnel.

"The chili is headed our way!" shouted Larryboy. "Run for it!"

They hadn't gone very far when a wall of glowing hot chili suddenly poured into the cavern, flooding the entire tunnel. There was no way they were going to outrun this wave of burning liquid.

But that's when they heard a voice. **"KAWABUNGA, BABY!"**

It was Tourist-Man. He was on a surfboard riding a wave of chili right toward them. Equally amazing, he had balanced his three pieces of luggage on his head.

"Hop on, dudes!" he shouted.

Tourist-Man's surfboard had two tiny engines strapped to its bottom. But even niftier, he steered the surfboard using a device that looked like the controls for a video game.

The Veggies scrambled up to a ledge and leaped aboard. They landed on top of the luggage, which was still balanced on Tourist-Man's head. However, Larryboy couldn't quite fit on the luggage, so he wound up on top of Bob.

They raced through the huge cavern looking like something from a circus act, scraping the ceiling as they went.

"Where did you get this surfboard?" Larryboy yelled over the roar of the rushing chili.

"It was in one of my suitcases!" Tourist-Man shouted back. "I carry doohickeys—they're what make me a superhero!"

"We're sorry we voted you off our side of the island," shouted Archie. "You didn't have to come back to rescue us, but you did. You're a true superhero, Tourist-Man!"

"Thanks!"

Then the surfing Veggies hit a big dip as the river of chili roared downhill.

"AHHHHHHHHHHHHHHHHHHHHH!"

It was like being on an amusement park ride gone berserk. A sharp right turn nearly toppled Larryboy from the top of the stack. If he hadn't fired a suction cup onto Bob's shiny head, Larryboy would have gone flying off and hit the wall.

"Oh my," Archie said, looking down at the surfboard.

"Oh my," was right. Archie was the first to notice that the acid-hot chili was slowly eating away at the surfboard. The board was now about one-third its original size.

Making things even more complicated, the cave narrowed up ahead with stalactites hanging from the ceiling like razor-sharp needles.

Larryboy had no choice. He had to leap from the top of Bob's head to keep from being shish-kebabed on the end of one of the daggerlike rocks. Still connected to Bob's head by his supersuction plunger, Larryboy wound up being pulled behind.

When Tourist-Man took a sharp left, Larryboy was flung around like the tail end in a crack-the-whip game. His tether cord wrapped around a stalactite, caught, and then ripped the deadly rock from the ceiling.

Bob ducked as the stalactite went whistling over his head, followed close behind by Larryboy.

"Hi, Bob! Bye, Bob," chirped Larryboy as he sailed just inches over Bob's noggin.

By this time, the chili had eaten away even more of the surfboard. It was now about half its original size—barely big enough to hold the Veggies.

"I think we're past the worst of it!" shouted Archie.

Wrong!

Just then, the volcano erupted.

KA-BLOOEY!

CHAPTER 16

HOT, HOT, HOT!

A geyser of chili lifted the tiny surfboard, pushing it up, up, up through a vertical shaft in the volcano. Larryboy, still attached to Bob's head by his plunger, trailed close behind.

"Top floor, please," Tourist-Man said, as if in an elevator, shooting up through a tall building.

A second later, the angry mountain spit them out of its top, hurling them high into the air. Of course, what goes up must come down. But it was a long way down!

"We're goners," yelled Bob, as their free fall began.

"Never say goner when I've still got luggage handy," said Tourist-Man, completely unruffled.

He pushed a button on his remote control, and his second piece of luggage popped open. Inside, a hang glider automatically unfolded.

The group clutched onto the glider as Tourist-Man steered it through a shower of erupting chili and blobs of sizzling hot cheese, which shot from the top of Mount Superhero.

Down on the island, the exclusive resort was in flames. None of the superheroes cared any longer who was First or Second Class, who was a servant, or who had what special powers.

Disasters have a way of putting everyone in the same boat—in this case, a sinking boat.

Lava-hot chili consumed buildings in its fiery flow. Giant, stale dinner rolls crashed through roofs. Shredded cheese fell from on high like gooey ash, gunking up everything in sight.

The island looked like a giant food fight.

By this time, most of the superheroes had attempted to escape by boat, helicopter, plane, jet-pack, or by simply flying on their own steam. But every one of them hit an invisible force field—like birds flying into a windowpane.

They were trapped on Superhero Island.

Tourist-Man brought the hang glider down in a cove, which just happened to be the spot where Coconut was waiting for Chili Pepper.

"Stay right where you are, Coconut!" shouted Larryboy, running toward the thug. "We know Chili Pepper was behind this volcanic eruption! So tell us how to get off this island. You and the Snooty Gourmet must have an escape route."

Coconut didn't say a word.

Larryboy aimed a supersuction ear at the hooligan. "If you don't tell us, I've got a chili-filled plunger with your name on it."

"Okay, okay," said Coconut. "I'll tell you anything, but please no more chili! I've had enough!"

"How do we get off the island?" Larryboy repeated.

"There's a hole in the invisible force field about 100 feet below the surface of the ocean and about a half mile away from this beach."

Coconut handed a map to Larryboy, showing exactly how to locate the underwater hole in the force field. "Here, I won't need it anyway. Chili and I don't have a way to reach the escape hole anymore."

"You didn't plan your escape very carefully," said

Larryboy. "You've trapped yourselves on the island, too."

"Our escape pod was stolen by a huge rock with angry eyes," grumbled Coconut. "Now can I leave? I think Chili is still somewhere on the island. I've got to find him!"

"Sure, go ahead."

As Coconut took off for the center of the burning island, the group was left with two burning questions: How were they going to reach the hole in the force field if it was deep underwater? And how were they going to save the other superheroes?

All eyes turned to Tourist-Man, who had one piece of luggage left.

CHAPTER 17

THERE'S A HOLE
IN THE BOTTOM OF THE SEA

"Of course I have scuba gear," said Tourist-Man matter-of-factly. "I also have a submersible jet ski. Will that help?"

With another push of a button, Tourist-Man's third piece of luggage popped open, revealing a submersible jet ski and miniature breathing tanks.

"Who says that heroes who use doohickeys and gadgets aren't important?" said Vicki, with a big grin.

"Right-O!" smiled Larryboy. "Here's the plan, guys. Tourist-Man, can you use the map and your doohickeys to get Bob, Vicki, and Archie safely through the hole in the force field?"

"Yes," agreed Tourist-Man. "But aren't you coming with us?"

Larryboy tried to strike a dramatic pose, but it was hard to do when little streams of chili were pouring onto the beach. He kept dancing around the sizzling streams.

"Drat," said Larryboy. "Forget the dramatic pose. I'm heading back to the center of the island. Someone needs to tell the other superheroes how to get out of here! We've got to include them in our plan!"

"You're willing to do that for superheroes who thought they were better than you all week?" Archie asked. "A lot of people wouldn't be willing to risk their necks for people like that."

"EVERYONE is just as important as the other in God's eyes. And I don't have a neck," Larryboy pointed out.

"That's the spirit!" Archie beamed.

Then Larryboy recited the words from the Superhero Handbook: "Don't be proud. Be willing to be a friend of people who aren't considered important. Don't think you are better than others."

With that, Larryboy dashed to the center of the inferno, knowing full well that he might be giving up his only hope of escape.

CHAPTER 18

TARZAN OF THE VEGGIES

Burning-hot chili was everywhere. In fact, once Larryboy got past the beach, the edge of the jungle was as far as he could go. The entire jungle floor was covered with chili. There was no way to get past the hot liquid to the resort, where the other superheroes were trapped.

Unless…

"Tarzan, eat your heart out!" Larryboy yelled.

Larryboy used his supersuction ears to leap from branch to branch in the tropical rain forest. **"AHHHH-U-AHHHHH-U-AHHHHH-U…ACK!"** he coughed as he tried to do the Tarzan yell, nearly choking on smoke gushing out of the volcano.

At the resort, Larryboy located the Larrymobile, but he found it covered in a thick layer of melted cheese.

"Drat," the caped cucumber said.

"Need some help?" said a voice.

Larryboy looked up to see Lemon Twist. Behind her were his old pals, the Scarlet Tomato, Electro-Melon, and Sweet Potato.

"Sorry we acted like we were more important than ya'll this week," said Sweet Potato, with Electro-Melon and Lemon Twist nodding in agreement.

"The same-a here," added the Scarlet Tomato.

"I guess it's easy to think you're better than others. But the fact is, we're not," added Electro-Melon.

"Thanks," said Larryboy. "But we don't have much time. Can you guys help me get this cheese off the Larrymobile?"

"My uncle Guido could-a probably eat all of that-a cheese," said the Scarlet Tomato. "But he's-a on a low-fat diet now, and my-a aunt Laverne wouldn't-a let him even look at this-a much cheese-a. He tries-a to raid the refrigerator every night, which is why—"

"Sorry, S.T., but we don't have time to hear about it," said Lemon Twist. Without another word, the twisting lemon powered up her tornado winds and literally blew the cheese off of the Larrymobile.

"Thanks, Lemon Twist," said Larryboy. "Now, here's my plan..."

Twenty minutes later, Larryboy and the other 133 superheroes were crowded onto one of the last remaining pieces of island not covered with hot chili or cheese. Wearing scuba gear borrowed from the resort's sport shop, the superheroes were connected to the Larrymobile by 133 water-ski ropes.

"Can the Larrymobile pull this many water-skiers at the same time?" asked Sweet Potato.

"Time to find out," said Electro-Melon.

Larryboy pushed a yellow button on his control panel, and the Larrymobile instantly transformed into the Larryboat. The purple speedboat tore off across the burning chili with 133 superheroes trailing behind—each one trying to water-ski on chili without getting their ropes tangled or their costumes fried.

Larryboy raced straight for the ocean. As he did, the entire island began to snap, crackle, and pop. The chili was so hot that it ate away at the water skis. But just before the Larryboat and the skiers became completely cooked, they reached the cool, refreshing water of the ocean.

At the edge of the sea, Larryboy pushed the orange button, and the Larrymobile changed from a boat to a submarine. Diving beneath the surface of the sea, the Larrysubmarine continued to pull the water-skiers along. Only they were now *underwater skiers* using their scuba gear.

As the Larrysubmarine raced through the underwater hole in the force field, Superhero Island sank into the sea and completely vanished from sight.

It was gone. **KAPUT!**

It was almost as if Superhero Island had never even existed.

CHAPTER 19

SOMETHING'S R.O.T.T.E.N.

Three days

later, back in Bumblyburg, in a secret

hideout beneath the Bumble Hotel, one

of the most dastardly meetings of all time

was being held. It was the monthly meeting

of that exclusive but diabolical club known as

R.O.T.T.E.N.—the League of Really Ornery and

Terribly Tacky Evildoers who are very Naughty.

The most infamous villains in all of Veggiedom

were there, including Awful Alvin and his sidekick

Lampy, Outback Jack, the Emperor, the Alchemist and

Mother Pearl, Greta Von Gruesome, and the Iceberg and

his Snow Peas.

The mysterious rock was also there. In fact,

this creature was in the process of asking to be

admitted as a new member of the R.O.T.T.E.N.

Club. And that wasn't easy. You had to be a really rotten vegetable.

Which raised a good question. Should they let a rock monster join a club for vegetables only?

"So I lured all of the superheroes to my island by playing up to their pride," the boulder explained in his speech to the League Membership Committee. "I told the superheroes they should spend their vacation on an exclusive island specially designed for the best of the best—themselves! They bought it—hook, line, and sinker!"

The R.O.T.T.E.N. committee members nodded, smiled, and snickered.

"But how did you handle that meddling cucumber Larryboy?" asked Mother Pearl.

"That was easy," said the rock. "I separated Larryboy from the other heroes by sending him to the Second Class beach—a beach for superheroes without special powers. I figured he couldn't cause trouble if he was cut off from the others."

The villains exchanged smiles of approval.

"Once the superheroes were at my resort, I triggered a force field that trapped them on the island. And then I set off a volcanic eruption that would've made Mount Vesuvius seem like a picnic. Now I am happy to announce that over 130 superheroes have all been destroyed!"

A gasp arose from the villains on the R.O.T.T.E.N. committee.

"I was wondering where all of the superheroes were hiding the past week," said Awful Alvin. "This is cause for a celebration! Dance with me, Lampy!"

"Does that mean I'm evil enough for your organization?" the rock asked proudly. "Can a boulder join the rancid ranks of R.O.T.T.E.N.?"

The Emperor, a small but powerful cherry tomato, banged a gavel on the table. "Anyone who can do what you have just done deserves to be a member of R.O.T.T.E.N.—even if you are a rock. All in favor of making him a member give an evil cackle."

Every single villain responded with an evil cackle.

The Emperor banged his gavel once again. "It's unanimous. Rocky, you are the newest member of the exclusive R.O.T.T.E.N. Club. Bring out the food, and let's party!"

From a back room, a tall waiter wheeled out a huge platter of food covered with a silver lid.

"A toast to the end of all superheroes!" shouted the

Emperor, holding up his glass of soda.

"And a toast to the ARREST of all supervillains!" came another voice. However, this voice came from under the lid of the food platter.

The waiter lifted the lid, revealing none other than LARRYBOY. The plunger-headed hero raised a piece of toast in the air and then sprang into action. He fired a plunger at the boulder, while superheroes poured into the room from all sides.

Some superheroes crashed through the ceiling, sliding down on ropes. Others popped out of closets. Still others leaped out of the air duct vents in the walls.

"I thought you said you destroyed every superhero?" Iceberg shouted at the rock.

"I did!" blasted back the boulder. "You have to believe me!"

"Why should anyone believe you?" declared Larryboy. "You aren't even who you say you are."

Then, in the most dramatic moment of all, Larryboy used one of his supersuction ears to reveal that the rock monster was simply wearing a costume. Yanking off the costume was a stunning surprise!

Inside was none other than Chili Pepper.

CHAPTER 20

A PICTURE-PERFECT POSTCARD ENDING

The raid on **R.O.T.T.E.N.** set the record for the largest number of supervillain arrests in a single day. To celebrate a few weeks later, Tourist-Man invited all of the superheroes to his home to watch his slide show of vacation pictures. Over 100 superheroes gathered to watch his slides. Roughly 80 of them, however, were sound asleep.

"How can Tourist-Man make *this* vacation seem boring?" Vicki whispered.

"I don't know. Just his special talent, I guess," Larry the Janitor said.

The vacation on Superhero Island had included defusing bombs, surfing on hot lava-chili, being hurled out of an erupting volcano, and escaping through an underwater passage. But somehow, some way, Tourist-Man's slides were still dreadfully dull.

"And this is me buttoning my shirt," he said, showing a photo of his Hawaiian shirt. "And this is a close-up of the button. And here's…"

"By the way, where's Larryboy?" asked Vicki when the slide show mercifully came to an end.

"Gee, that's a good question."

Vicki had invited Larry the Janitor to be her escort to the party, since they never did get a chance to finish their picnic together. So our cucumber hero came as Larry, not Larryboy.

At first, Tourist-Man wasn't going to let Larry the Janitor come to the party, since—after all—he wasn't a superhero. But then Tourist-Man remembered what it was like to be left out. So he welcomed Larry with open arms (or at least he would've if he had arms).

"Larryboy's not here. So I guess you're just stuck with me—an unimportant janitor," Larry said to Vicki.

"Unimportant janitor? How can you say that? EVERYONE is important in God's eyes," Vicki responded. And then she gave him a big grin. "Besides, you're just the way I like you."

Larry the Janitor beamed.

At that moment, Sweet Potato leaned over and said, "Hey, I never did hear how ya'll figured out that Chili Pepper disguised himself as a rock."

"It was his breath," Vicki said. "Larryboy realized that Chili Pepper's bad breath was just like the dangerously spicy breath of the mysterious rock."

"But why did Chili Pepper even need a disguise?" asked Sweet Potato.

"Because Chili desperately wanted to become a member of R.O.T.T.E.N.," interjected Bob the Tomato.

"That's right," said Vicki. "Bob and I discovered that about a year ago, Chili Pepper tried to join the R.O.T.T.E.N. Club, but they wouldn't let him in. They said he wasn't evil enough to join their club. Being left out like that, he felt really rejected."

"So Chili Pepper came up with the boulder disguise and devised the most evil plot he could think of—destroying almost every superhero in the world with something he loved the most," said Bob. "If that didn't get him into the R.O.T.T.E.N. Club, nothing would."

"His plot had one other advantage," added Vicki. "Chili thought that Coconut would ruin his chances of making it into the R.O.T.T.E.N. Club. So he decided to ditch

Coconut by disguising himself as a rock and abandoning his sidekick on the island."

"The disguise also gave him a secret identity to use while he was stealing scuba gear and other supplies for his resort," Bob noted.

"Diabolical," gasped Sweet Potato. "I wonder what ever happened to Coconut."

Good question.

For an answer, let's go to the other side of Bumblyburg, where Chili Pepper was locked away in the Jail for the Criminally Snobby. On this particular day, one of the prison guards had brought him a particularly odd postcard.

"Mail for Chili Pepper!" announced the guard, sneaking a peek at the postcard.

"Give that to me," Chili Pepper snarled, snatching it from the guard. Burning with curiosity, Chili flipped over the postcard, and this is what he read:

Dear Chili:

Weather is good. Wish you were here. I just wanted to give you my great news. When Superhero Island sank into the ocean, I SURVIVED!

When the island sank, I climbed onto a giant dinner roll and drifted at sea for a week before being picked up by a ship. So don't worry. I'll be waiting for you when you get out of jail. See you soon!

Your sidekick and faithful friend,

Coconut

Coconut was back? Chili Pepper couldn't believe it. His eyes bulged. Steam came out of his ears. He turned red in the face. And then...

"AHHHHHHHHHHHHHHHHHHHHHHHHHHH!"

Chili Pepper exploded in anger. He flipped his lid.

You might even say he erupted.

THE END

We want to hear from you. Please send your comments about this book to us in care of zreview@zondervan.com. Thank you.

ZONDERVAN.com/
AUTHORTRACKER
follow your favorite authors